Why was his hand still moving toward her hair?

Just in time, he pulled it back. That wouldn't do at all.

Sam was getting a little too interested in Susan. She was totally wrong for him in the long-term, even though she was turning out to be an amazing summer nanny. He needed to find Mindy a permanent mom. And he needed to do it soon.

He'd make sure to get back on the dating circuit right away. He just needed to get himself motivated to do it. He'd been too busy. But now that Susan was in place—Susan, who was completely inappropriate for him—he'd jump back into pursuing that all-important goal.

He forced himself to take a step backward. "If you're interested in the extra job of planning my company picnic, I'd appreciate having you do it. It would be easy, because you're here in the house anyway. But if you're not comfortable with it, I'll find someone else."

She studied him, quizzical eyes on his face. "I can give it a try," she said slowly.

Sam tried to ignore the sudden happiness surging through him.

Lee Tobin McClain read *Gone with the Wind* in the third grade and has been a hopeless romantic ever since. When she's not writing angst-filled love stories with happy endings, she's getting inspiration from her church singles group, her gymnastics-obsessed teenage daughter and her rescue dog and cat. In her day job, Lee gets to encourage aspiring romance writers in Seton Hill University's low-residency MFA program. Visit her at leetobinmcclain.com.

Books by Lee Tobin McClain

Love Inspired

Rescue River

Engaged to the Single Mom
His Secret Child
Small-Town Nanny

Small-Town Nanny

Lee Tobin McClain

Recycling programs
for this product may
not exist in your area.

LOVE INSPIRED BOOKS

ISBN-13: 978-0-373-81917-1

Small-Town Nanny

www.Harlequin.com

Printed in U.S.A.

For I know the plans I have for you, declares the Lord, plans to prosper you and not to harm you, plans to give you hope and a future.
—*Jeremiah* 29:11

To the real Bob Eakin.
Thank you for your service.

Chapter One

Sam Hinton was about to conclude one of the biggest business deals of his career. And get home in time to read his five-year-old daughter her bedtime story.

He'd finally gotten the hang of being a single dad who happened to run a multimillion-dollar business.

Feeling almost relaxed for the first time since his wife's death two years ago, Sam surveyed the only upscale restaurant in his small hometown of Rescue River, Ohio, with satisfaction. He'd helped finance this place just to have an appropriate spot to bring important clients, and it was bustling. He recognized his former high school science teacher coming through the door. There was town matriarch Miss Minnie Falcon calling for her check in her stern, Sunday-school-teacher voice. At a table by the window, one of the local farmers laughed with his teenage kids at what looked to be a graduation dinner.

And who was that new, petite, dark-haired waitress? Was it his sister's friend Susan Hayashi?

Sam tore his eyes away from the pretty server and checked his watch, wondering how long a visit to the men's room could take his client. The guy must be either checking with his board of directors or playing some kind of game with Sam—seeming to back off, hoping to drag down the price of the agricultural property he was buying just a little bit more before he signed on the dotted line. Fine. Sam would give a little if it made his client's inner tightwad happy.

Crash!

"Leave her alone! Hands off!" The waitress he'd noticed, his sister's friend Susan, left the tray and food where she'd dropped them and stormed across the dining room toward his client.

Who stood leering beside another, very young-looking, waitress. "Whoa, hel-lo, baby!" his client said to Susan as she approached.

"Don't get jealous. I'm man enough for both of you ladies!"

"Back *off*!"

Sam shoved out of his chair and headed toward the altercation. Around him, people were murmuring with concern or interest.

"It's okay, Susan," the teenage waitress was saying to his sister's friend. "He d-d-didn't really hurt me."

Stepping protectively in front of the round-faced teenager, Susan pointed a delicate finger at his client. "You apologize to her," she ordered, poking the much larger, much older businessman in the chest with each word. She wore the same dark skirt and white blouse as all the other wait staff, but her almond-shaped eyes and high cheekbones made her stand out almost as much as her stiff posture and flaring nostrils. Three or four gold hoops quivered in each ear.

"Keep your hands off me." Sam's client sneered down at Susan. "Where's the owner of this place? I don't have to put up with anything from a…" He lowered his voice, but whatever he said made the color rise in Susan's face.

Sam clapped a hand on his client's shoulder. He hadn't pegged the guy as this much of a troublemaker, but then, he barely knew him. "Come on. Leave the ladies alone."

The other man glanced at Sam and changed his tone. "Aw, hey, I was just trying to have a good time." He gave Susan another dirty look. "Some girls can't take a joke."

"Some jokes aren't funny, mister." She glared at him, two high spots of color staining her cheeks pink.

The restaurant manager rushed up behind them. "We can work this out. Mr. Hinton, I do apologize. You girls…" He clapped his hands at the two waitresses. "My office. Now."

"I'm so sorry, I didn't mean to cause trouble!" Crying, the teenage waitress hurried toward the office at the back of the restaurant.

Susan touched the manager's arm. "Don't get mad at Tawny. I'm the one who got in Prince Charming's face." She jerked her head sideways toward Sam's client.

The restaurant manager frowned and ushered Susan to his office.

Sam's client shrugged and gave Sam a conspiratorial grin as he turned toward their table. "Ready to get back to business?"

"No," Sam said, frowning after the restaurant manager and Susan. "We're done here."

"What?" His client's voice rose to a squeak.

"I'll see you to your car. I want you out of Rescue River."

Ten minutes later, after he'd banished his would-be client, settled the bill and fixed things with the restaurant manager, Sam strode out to the parking lot.

There was Susan, standing beside an ancient, rusty subcompact, staring across the moonlit fields that circled the town of Rescue River. He'd only met her a couple of times; unfortunately, he worked too much to get to know his sister's friends.

"Hey, Susan," he called as he approached. "I got you your job back."

She half turned and arched an eyebrow. "Oh, you did, did you? Thanks, but no thanks."

"Really?" He stopped a few yards away from her. Although he hadn't expected gratitude, exactly, the complete dismissal surprised him.

"Really." She crossed her arms and leaned back against her car. "I don't need favors from anyone."

"It's not a favor, it's just…fairness."

"It's a favor, and I don't want it. You think I can go back in there and earn tips after the scene I just made?"

"You probably could." Not only was she

attractive, but she appeared to be very competent, if a little on the touchy side. "Rescue River doesn't take kindly to men being jerks. Most of the people in that room were squarely on your side."

"Wait a minute." Her eyes narrowed as she studied him. "Now I get it. You're part owner of the place."

"I'm a silent partner, yes." He cocked his head to one side, wondering where this was going.

"You're trying to avoid a sexual harassment lawsuit, aren't you?"

His jaw dropped. "Really? You think that's why…" He trailed off, rubbed the heavy stubble on his chin, and thought of his daughter, waiting for him at home. "Look, if you don't want the job back, that's fine. And if you think you have a harassment case, go for it."

"Don't worry. It wasn't me your buddy was groping, and I'm not the lawsuit type." She sighed. "Probably not the waitress type either, like Max said when he was firing me."

Sam felt one side of his mouth quirk up in a smile as he recognized the truth of that statement. He found Susan to be extremely cute, with her long, silky hair, slender figure and vaguely Asian features, but she definitely wasn't the eager-to-please type.

Wasn't *his* type, not that it mattered. He preferred soft-spoken women, domestic ladies who wore makeup and perfume and knew how to nurture a man. Archaic, but there it was.

Just then, the teenage waitress came rushing out through the kitchen door. "Susan, you didn't have to do that! Max said he fired you. I'm sorry!"

"No big deal." She shrugged again, the movement a little stiff.

"But I thought you needed the money to send your brother to that special camp—"

"It's fine." Susan's voice wobbled the tiniest bit, or was he imagining it? "Just, well, don't let guys do that kind of stuff to you."

"I know, I know, but I didn't want to get in trouble. Especially with Mr. Hinton on the premises…" The girl trailed off, realizing for the first time that Sam stood to one side, listening to every word. "Oh, I didn't know you were there! Don't be mad at her, Mr. Hinton. She was just trying to help me!"

Susan patted her on the shoulder. "Go back inside and remember, just step on a guy's foot—hard—if he tries anything. You can always claim it was an accident."

"That's a great idea! You're totally awesome!" The younger woman gave Susan a quick hug and then trotted back into the restaurant.

Susan let her elbows drop to the hood of her car and rested her chin in her hands. "Was I ever that young?"

"Don't talk like you're ancient. What are you, twenty-five, twenty-six?" Susan was relatively new in town, and if memory served, she was a teacher at the elementary school. Apparently waitressing on the side. Sam assumed she was about his sister Daisy's age, since they'd fast become thick as thieves.

"Good guess, *Mr.* Hinton. You didn't even need your bifocals to figure that out. I'm twenty-five."

Okay, at thirty-seven he *was* a lot older than she was, but her jibe stung. Maybe because he knew very well that he wasn't getting any younger and that he needed to get cracking on his next major life goal.

Which would involve someone a lot softer and gentler than Susan Hayashi. "Listen," he said, "I'm sorry about what happened. You should know that guy who caused the trouble is headed back toward the east coast even as we speak. And he's not my friend, by the way. Just a client. Former client, now."

She arched a delicate brow. "My knight in shining armor, are you?"

What was there to say to a woman who misinterpreted his every move? He shook his head, reached out to pat her shoulder, then decided it wasn't a good idea and pulled his hand back. If he touched her, she might report him. Or throw a punch.

Definitely a woman to steer clear of.

There didn't seem to be any sweetness in her. So it surprised Sam when, as he bid her goodnight, he caught a whiff of honeysuckle perfume.

The next day, even though she wanted to pull the covers over her head and cry, Susan forced herself to climb out of bed early. She'd committed to spend her Saturday morning helping at the church's food pantry, and honestly, even that might not have gotten her out of bed, but she knew her best friend, Daisy, was going to be there.

"Come on," Daisy said when Susan dragged herself down the steps and into the church basement, "we're doing produce. Hey, did you really get fired last night?"

Embarrassment heated Susan's face as she followed her friend to an out-of-the-way corner where bins of spinach and lettuce donated by local farmers stood ready to be divided into smaller bunches. "Yeah. How'd you hear?"

"That sweet little Tawny Thompson spread it all over town, how you rescued her from some creepy businessman. What were you thinking?"

"He practically had his hand up her skirt! What was I supposed to do?"

"I don't know, tell the manager? Honestly, I would've done the same thing, but I'm not in your position. You needed that job!"

"I know." Susan blew out a sigh as she studied the wooden crates of leafy greens. Her hopes of funding the summer respite her mom needed so desperately had flown out the window last night. "Waitressing at a nice restaurant like Chez La Ferme is definitely the best money I can make, but I get so mad at guys like that. I thought Max would back me up, not fire me."

"Can you even send your brother to camp now?"

"Probably not. I shouldn't have told him he could go, but when I landed this waitressing job and found out it could be full-time as soon as school lets out for the summer, I thought I had the fee easy. I had a payment plan, everything. Now…" She focused on lettuce bunches so Daisy wouldn't see the tears in her eyes.

"What are you going to do?"

"I don't know. And to top it off, I might have to move home for the summer." Even saying it made her heart sink. She loved Rescue River and had all kinds of plans for her summer here.

"Why? You're always talking about how you and your mom…"

"Don't get along? Yeah." She sighed, wishing it wasn't so, wishing she had a storybook family like so many of the Midwestern ones she saw around her these days. "I love Mom, but she and I are like oil and water. If I go back, honestly, it'll stress her out more. I just want—*wanted*—her to have a summer to garden and antique shop with her friends, maybe even go on a few dates, without worrying about Donny."

An older couple wandered over. "You guys okay? Need any help?"

"We've got it." Daisy waved them away and carried a load of bagged lettuce to a sorting table. "So you had a good plan. But you couldn't help what happened."

"I could have been more…refined about it."

A couple of tears overflowed, and Susan took off her plastic gloves to dig in her pocket for a tissue. "When am I ever going to learn to control my temper?" She blew her nose.

Daisy put an arm around her. "When you turn into a whole different person. You know, God made you the way you are, and He has a plan for you. Something will work out." She paused. "Why would you move back home, anyway? What's wrong with your room at Lacey's?"

"Lacey's got renovation fever." Susan pulled on a fresh pair of plastic gloves. "Remember, she gave me my room cheap because she knew I'd have to move when she started fixing up the place. So now her brother—you know Buck, right? Well, he's dried out and ready to help, and summer's the best time for them to get going." She gauged the right amount of lettuce for a family of four, put it in a plastic bag and twist-tied it. "And I don't have money for a deposit on a new place. I'll need to save up."

"You can stay with me. You know that."

"You're sweet." Susan side-hugged her friend. "And you live in a tiny place with two dogs and a cat. You have exactly zero room, except in that big heart of yours."

Daisy pried open another crate, this one full of kale leaves. "We just have to pray about it."

"Well, pray fast, because Lacey asked if I could be out next week. And even if I can land a job at another restaurant in Rescue River—which I doubt, with the non-recommendation Max is giving me—I won't be making anything like the tips I could bring in at Chez Le Ferme." She sighed as she dumped out the last of the kale leaves and stowed the wooden crate under the table. "I'm such an idiot."

"I've got it!" Daisy snapped her fingers, a smile lighting her plump face. "I know exactly what you can do for the summer!"

"What?" Susan eyed her friend dubiously and then went back to bagging kale. Daisy was wonderful, but she tended to get overexcited when she had a new idea.

"You know my brother Sam, right? He was at the Easter service at church, and at Troy and Angelica's wedding."

"I remember. In fact, he was at the restaurant last night. He...actually said he could get me my job back, but I turned him down." Susan felt her face flush as she thought of their conversation. She'd still been heated about the encounter with that jerk of a businessman, and she hadn't had her guard up around Daisy's brother, as she had the previous couple of times they'd met. She had the distinct feeling she'd been rude to him, but truthfully, he'd disconcerted her with his dominant-guy effort to make all her problems go away.

He was a handsome man, no doubt of that. Tall and broad-shouldered, an all-American quarterback type with a square jaw and close-cropped dark hair.

But he was one of those super traditional guys, she could just tell. In fact, he reminded her of her father, who thought women belonged in the home, not the workplace. Dad had wanted his wife to stay home, and Mom had, and look where it had gotten her. To make matters worse, her father had expected Susan to do the same, sending her to college only for her MRS degree, which she obviously hadn't gotten. Which she had no interest in getting, not now, not ever. She was a career woman with a distinct calling to teach kids, especially those with special needs. Susan wasn't one of those people who heard clear instructions from God every week or two, but in the case of her life's work, she'd gotten the message loud and clear.

Daisy waved her hand impatiently. "You don't want that job back. I have a better idea.

Did I tell you how Sam hired a college girl to take care of Mindy over the summer?"

"What?" Susan pulled herself back to the present, rubbed the back of her plastic-gloved hand over her forehead and tried to focus on what Daisy was saying.

"Sam texted me this morning, all frantic. That girl he hired to be Mindy's summer nanny just let him know late last night that she can't do it. She got some internship in DC or something. Now Sam's hunting for someone to take her place. You'd be perfect!"

Susan laughed in disbelief. "I'd be a disaster! I'm a terrible cook, and…what do nannies even do, anyway?" She had some impression of them as paid housewives, and that was the last thing she wanted to be.

"You're great with kids! You're a teacher. Do you know Mindy?"

Susan nodded. "Cute kid, but sort of notorious for playground fights. I've bailed her out a few times."

"She can be a bit of a terror. Losing her mom was hard, and then Sam hasn't been able to keep a babysitter or nanny…"

"And why would that be?" Susan knew the answer without even asking. You could tell from spending two minutes with Sam that he was a demanding guy.

"He works a lot of hours and he expects a lot. Not so much around the house, he has a cleaning service, but he's very particular about how Mindy is taken care of. And then with Mindy being temperamental and, um, *spirited*, it's not been easy for the people Sam has hired. But you'd be absolutely perfect!"

"Daisy, think." Susan raised a brow at her friend. "I just got fired for being too mouthy and for not putting up with baloney from chauvinistic guys. And you think this would be perfect how?"

Daisy looked crestfallen for a minute, and then her face brightened. "The thing is, deep inside, Sam would rather have someone who stands up to him than someone who's a marshmallow. Just look how well he gets along with me!"

Susan chuckled and lifted another crate to the table. "You're his little sister. He has to put up with you."

"Sam's nuts about me because I don't let him get away with his caveman attitude. You wouldn't, either. But that's not the point."

"Okay, what's the point?" Susan couldn't help feeling a tiny flicker of hope about this whole idea—it would be so incredible to be able to send Donny to camp, not to disappoint him and her mother yet again—but she tamped it down. There was no way this would work from either end, hers or Sam's.

"The point is," Daisy said excitedly, "you're certified in special education. That's absolutely amazing! There's no way Sam could say you don't know what you're doing!"

"Uh-huh." Susan felt that flicker again.

"He'll pay a lot. And the thing is, you can live in! You'll have the summer to save up for a deposit on a new place."

Susan drew in a breath as the image of her mother and autistic brother flickered again in her mind. "But Daisy," she said gently, "Sam doesn't like me. When we talked last night, I could tell."

One of the food pantry workers came over. "Everything okay here, ladies?"

"Oh, sure, of course! We just got to talking! Sorry!"

For a few minutes, they focused on their produce, efficiently filling bags with kale and then more leaf lettuce, pushing a cartload of bundles over to the distribution tables, coming back to bag up sugar snap peas and radishes someone had dumped in a heap on their table.

Working with the produce felt soothing to Susan. She'd grown up urban and gotten most of her vegetables at the store, but she remembered occasional Saturday trips to the farmers market with her mother, Donny in tow.

Her mother had tried so hard to please her dad, who, with his Japanese ancestry, liked eggplant and cucumbers and napa cabbage. She and her mom had watched cooking videos together, and her mom had studied cookbooks and learned to be a fabulous Japanese chef. Susan's mouth watered just thinking about daikon salad and salt-pickled cabbage and broccoli stir-fry.

But had it worked? Had her dad been happy? Not really. He'd always had some kind of criticism, and her mother would sneak off and cry and try to do better, and it was never good enough. And as she and Donny had grown up, they hadn't been enough either, and Susan knew her mother had blamed herself. Having given birth to a rebellious daughter and a son with autism, she felt she'd failed as a woman.

Her mom's perpetual guilt had ended up making Susan feel guilty, too, and as a hormonal teenager, she'd taken those bad feelings out on her mother. And then Dad had left them, and the sense of failure had been complete.

Susan shook off the uncomfortable reminder of her own inadequacy and looked around. Where was Daisy?

Just then, her friend stood up from rummaging in her purse, cell phone in hand. "I'm calling Sam and telling him to give you an interview."

"No!" Panic overwhelmed Susan. "Don't do it!" She dropped the bundle of broccoli she was holding and headed toward Daisy. There was no way she could interview with a man who reminded her so much of her father.

"You can't stop me!" Daisy teased, and then, probably seeing the alarm on Susan's face, put her phone behind her and held out a hand. "Honey, God works in mysterious ways, but I am totally sensing this is a God thing. Just let me do it. Just do an interview and see what he says, see how you guys get along."

Susan felt her life escaping from her control. "I don't—"

"You don't have to take the job. Just do the interview."

"But what if—"

"Please? I'm your friend. I have no vested interest in how this turns out. Well, except for keeping you in town."

"I…" Susan felt her will to resist fading.

There was a lot that was good about the whole idea, right? And so what if it was uncomfortable for her? If her mom and Donny could be happy, she'd be doing her duty, just as her dad had asked her to do before he'd left. *You have to take care of them, Suzie,* her dad had said in his heavily accented English.

"I'm setting something up for this afternoon. If not sooner." Daisy turned back to the phone and Susan felt a sense of doom settling over her.

That afternoon, Susan climbed out of her car in front of Sam's modern-day mansion on the edge of Rescue River, grabbed her portfolio, and headed up the sidewalk, all the while arguing with God. "Daisy says You'll make a way where there is no way, but what if I don't like Your way? And I can say for sure that Sam Hinton isn't going to like *my* way, so this is a waste of time I could be—"

The double front doors swung open. She caught a glimpse of a high-ceilinged entryway, a mahogany table full of framed photos and a spectacular, sparkling chandelier, but it was Sam Hinton who commanded her attention. He stood watching her approach, wearing a sleeves-rolled-up white dress shirt and jeans, arms crossed, legs apart.

Talk about a man and his castle. And those arms! Was he a bodybuilder in his spare time or what?

"Thanks for coming." He extended one massive hand to her.

She reached out and shook it, ignoring the slight breathlessness she felt. This was Sam, Daisy's super-traditional businessman of a brother, not America's next male model. "No problem. Daisy thought it would be a good idea."

"Yes. She had me squeeze you in, but you should know that I'm interviewing several other candidates today."

"No problem." Was God going to let her off this easy?

"It seems like a lot of people are interested in the job, probably because I'm paying well for a summer position." He ushered her in.

"How well?"

He threw a figure over his shoulder as he led her into an oak-lined office in the front of the house, and Susan's jaw dropped.

Twice as much as she'd ever hoped to make waitressing. She could send Donny to camp and her mom to the spa. Maybe even pay for another graduate course.

Okay, God—and Daisy—You were right. It's the perfect job for me.

He gestured her into the seat in front of his broad oak desk, and Susan felt a pang of nostalgia. Her dad had done the exact same thing when he wanted to talk to her about some infraction of his rules. Only his desk had just been an old door on a couple of sawhorses in the basement. How he would have loved a home office like this one.

"I don't know if you've met Mindy, but she has some…limitations." His jaw jutted out as if he was daring her to make a comment.

"If you think of them that way." The words were out before she could weigh the wisdom of saying them, and she shouldn't have, but come on! The child was missing a hand, not a heart or a set of lungs.

Sam's eyebrows shot up. "I think I know my child better than you do. Have you even met Mindy?"

Rats, rats, rats. Would she ever learn to shut her big mouth? "I teach at Mindy's school, so I've been the recess and lunchroom monitor during her kindergarten year. I know about her hand. But of course, you know her better, you're her father."

Sam was eyeing her with a level glare.

"We have a sign up at school that reads, 'Argue for your limitations, and sure enough, they're yours.' I think it's Richard Bach. I just meant…it's an automatic response." *Stop talking, Susan.* God might have a nice plan for her, but she was perfectly capable of ruining nice plans. She'd done it all her life. She fumbled in her portfolio. "Here's my résumé."

He took it, glanced over it. Then looked more closely. "You've done coursework on physical disabilities? Graduate coursework?"

"Yeah. I'm working on my master's in special ed. Bit by bit."

"Why not go back full-time? At least summers? Why are you looking to work instead?"

"Quite frankly, I have a mother and brother to help support." *Hello, Mr. Rich Guy, everyone's not rolling in money like you are.*

"Doesn't the district pay for your extra schooling?"

"Six credits per year, which is two classes. I've used mine up."

He was studying her closely, as if she was a bug pinned on the wall. Or as if she was a woman he was interested in, but she was absolutely certain that couldn't be. "I see." He nodded. "Well, I'm not sure this would be the job for you anyway. I go out in the evenings pretty often."

"Really?" She opened her mouth to say more and then clamped it closed. *Shut up, you want this job.*

"I know, being young and adventurous, you must go out a lot yourself."

"Don't make assumptions. That's not what I was thinking." She looked away from him, annoyed.

"What were you thinking?"

"Do you really want to know?"

"Try me."

"I was thinking: you work super long hours, right? And you go out in the evenings. So… when do you spend time with your daughter?"

Sam stared at Susan as her question hung in the air between them. "When do I…? Look. If you've already decided I'm a terrible parent, this isn't going to work."

Truthfully, her words uncovered the guilt that consumed him as an overworked single dad. He hated how much time he had to spend away from Mindy. Half the time, he hated dating, too, but he'd promised Marie that he'd remarry so that Mindy wouldn't be raised without a mother in the home. Probably, she'd made him promise because she knew how much he worked and feared that Mindy would be raised by babysitters if he didn't remarry.

Well, he'd changed and was trying to change more, but he'd made a promise—not just about remarrying, but about what type of mom Mindy needed, actually—and he intended to keep it. Which didn't mean this snippy schoolteacher had the right to condemn him.

"Look, I'm sorry. It's not my place to judge and I don't know your situation. Ask Daisy, I'm way too outspoken and it always gets me into trouble." Her face was contrite and her apology sounded sincere. "The thing is, I know kids and I'm good with them. If you're struggling, either with her disability or with…other issues, I could help. Build up her self-esteem, encourage her independence." Those pretty, almond-shaped brown eyes looked a little bit shiny, as if she was holding back tears. "Don't turn me down just because I'm mouthy, if you think I'd be a help to Mindy."

She was right. And he was a marshmallow around women who looked sad, especially seriously cute ones like Susan. "It's okay."

And it *was* okay. He recognized already that his burst of anger had more to do with his own guilty feelings than with her comment. But that didn't mean he had to hire her.

The doorbell chimed, making them both jump. "That's probably my next interview. I'm sorry." He stood. "Here's your résumé back."

"It's all right, you can keep it. In case you change your mind." She stood and grabbed her elegant black portfolio. Come to think of it, all of her was elegant, from her close-fitting black trousers to her white shirt and vest to her long black hair with a trendy-looking stripe of red in it, neatly clipped back.

Just for a minute, he wondered what that hair would look like flowing free.

Sam forced that thought away as he came around his desk to Susan's side. She looked neat and professional, but as soon as she opened her mouth, it became apparent that she was quite a character. Sam shook his head as he ushered her through the entryway. Why Daisy had thought he and Susan could work together was beyond him.

Thinking about her interview, he couldn't help grinning. What job applicant questioned and insulted the potential boss? You didn't see that in the business world. He was used to people kowtowing to him, begging for a job. Susan could take a few lessons in decorum, but he had to admit he enjoyed her spunk.

The doorbell chimed again just as they reached it, so he was in the awkward position of having two job applicants pass each other in the doorway. The new one, a curvaceous blonde in a flowered dress, stood smiling, a plate of plastic-wrap-covered cookies in her hands.

"Hi, are you Mr. Hinton? Thank you so much for agreeing to interview me. I would just absolutely love to have this job! What a great house!"

"Come on in." He gestured the new applicant into the entryway. "Susan, I'll be in touch.'"

"I hope so," she murmured as she brushed past him and out the door. "But I'm not holding my breath."

Chapter Two

The next Thursday afternoon, Sam arrived at the turnoff to his brother Troy's farm with a sense of relief. His sister was right; he needed to take a break from interviewing nannies during the day and working late into the night to make up for it. But he was desperate; Mindy's last day of school had been Tuesday, and without a regular child care provider, he'd had to stay home or use babysitters who weren't necessarily up to par.

Mindy bounced in her booster seat. "There's the sign! Look, it says *D-O-G*, dog! But what else does it say, Daddy?"

He slowed to read the sign aloud: "A Dog's Last Chance: No-Cage Canine Rescue."

"Cuz Uncle Troy and Aunt Angelica and Xavier rescue dogs. Right?"

"That's right, sugar sprite." And he hoped they could rescue him, too. Or not rescue—they had too much going on for that—but at least give him ideas about getting a good child care provider for Mindy for the summer.

"There they are, there they are! And look, there's baby Emmie!"

Sure enough, his brother and sister-in-law stood outside the fenced kennel area. He parked, let Mindy out of the car and then paused to survey the scene.

Troy was reaching out for the baby, all of two weeks old, so that his wife could kneel down to greet Mindy with a huge hug.

The tableau they presented battered Sam's heart. He wanted this. He wanted a wife who would look up at him with that same loving, admiring expression Angelica gave Troy. Wanted a woman who'd embrace Mindy, literally and figuratively. Seeing how it thrilled Mindy, he even thought he wouldn't mind having another baby, a little brother or sister for them both to love.

This was what he and Marie had wanted, what they would have had, if God hadn't seen fit to grab it away from them.

He pushed the bitterness aside and strode

up to the happy family. "How's Emmie? She sleeping well?"

Troy and Angelica looked at each other and laughed. "Not a chance. We're up practically all night, every night," Troy said, and then Sam noticed the dark circles under his brother's eyes. Running a veterinary practice and a rescue while heading a family had to be exhausting, but though he looked tired, there was a deep happiness in Troy's eyes that hadn't been there before.

That was the power of love. Troy and Angelica had married less than a year ago and instantly conceived a baby, at least partly in response to Angelica's son Xavier's desire for a little sister. They'd even gotten the gender right.

Sam renewed his determination: With or without God's help, he was going to find this for himself and Mindy. He didn't need the Lord to solve his problems for him. He could do it on his own.

"Where's Xavier, Uncle Troy?"

Troy chuckled. "It's Kennel Kids day. Where do you think?"

For the first time, Sam noticed the cluster of boys on the far edge of the fenced area. It was the ragtag group of potential hoodlums that Troy mentored through giving them responsibilities at the kennel. Amazing that his brother, busy as he was, had time to work with kids in need. Or made time, truth be known, and Sam's conscience smote him. He ought to give more back to the community, but he felt as if he was barely holding his own life together these days. "Who's monitoring the boys? Is that Daisy?"

"Can I go play, Daddy?" Mindy begged.

"No."

"Why not?"

"It's not safe, honey."

"But Xavier's over there."

"Xavier's a boy, honey. And…" He broke off, seeing the knowing glance Troy and Angelica exchanged. Okay, so he was overprotective, but those boys were playing rough and Mindy, with her missing hand, had one less means of defense.

And one more reason to get teased, in the sometimes-cruel world of school-aged kids.

Mindy's face reddened and she drew in a breath, obviously about to have a major meltdown.

Sam squatted down beside her, touching her shoulder, willing her to stay calm. He was so tired after another late night working, and he wasn't that great about dealing with Mindy's frequent storms. Didn't know if there even was a good way to deal with them.

"Hey!" Angelica got a little bit in Mindy's face, startling her out of her intended shriek. "I know! Why don't you and your daddy go ask Xavier to take you down to the barn? He can show you the newest puppies. You can stay outside the fence," she added, rolling her eyes a little at Sam.

"Okay! C'mon, Daddy!"

Thank you, he mouthed to Angelica, bemused by the way a little girl's mood could change in a second.

"Not sure if you'll be thanking me in a minute," she said with a chuckle.

She must mean his ongoing battle with Mindy, the one where Angelica and Troy were staunchly on Mindy's side. "We're not getting a puppy!" he mouthed over his shoulder to Angelica, keeping his voice low so he wouldn't reawaken Mindy's interest in the issue.

But as he and Mindy approached the group at the other end of the fenced enclosure, Sam wondered if Angelica might have been talking with Daisy…and if her joke about him not thanking her might have meant something entirely different.

Because *she* was there.

Susan, the firebrand waitress and job candidate he hadn't been able to get out of his mind for the past four days.

Who was she to tell him he wasn't raising his daughter right?

And what on earth was she doing here?

The answer, apparently, was that she was working with the kids, because she was squatting down beside one of the smaller boys, probably seven or eight years old. From the boy's awkward movements, Troy guessed he had some kind of muscular disorder.

And Susan was helping him to pet a pit bull's face.

Sam shook his head. Of course she was. The woman obviously had no common sense, no safety consciousness, no awareness of what was age-appropriate. If that kid's parents could see what she was doing…of course, given the nature of Kennel Kids, the boy might not have involved parents. Still, Troy or Angelica ought to rein Susan in.

At that moment, she lifted her head and saw him. Her mouth dropped open, and then her eyes narrowed as if she was reading his mind.

"Xavier!" Mindy's joyous shout was a welcome distraction. "C'mere! C'mere!"

Susan called out to Daisy, who was, he now realized, standing guard over the overall group. Daisy came and knelt beside the boy Susan had been helping, and Susan exchanged a few heated words with her, then rose effortlessly to her feet. She followed Xavier, who was running toward the fence to see Mindy.

A knee-high black-and-white puppy bounded over on enormous, clumsy feet, barking. The kids immediately started playing with it, Mindy poking her fingers through the fence to touch its nose and Xavier jumping and rolling with the puppy on the inside of the enclosure. Which left Sam to watch Susan's approach. She wore cutoff shorts and a red shirt, hair up in a long ponytail. She looked young and innocent, especially since she'd removed her multiple earrings. "Didn't expect to see you here," he said, hoping his voice didn't betray his strange agitation.

"The feeling's mutual, and when I get the chance, I'm going to strangle your sister." She knelt down, and Xavier, along with the black-and-white dog, fell into her lap, pushing her backward.

Daisy. Oh. Susan's being here was Daisy's

doing. "I never could control that girl. She always does exactly what she wants."

She flashed a smile. "And she always means well."

He watched Susan struggle out from under the dog, laughing when it licked her face. Then she handed Xavier a ball from her shorts pocket and he threw it for the dog to fetch.

"What's Daisy doing?" Sam asked. "Is she pushing us together on purpose?" If his sister was playing matchmaker, she was doing a poor job of it. She had to know Susan wasn't his type, even though the thought of going out with Susan sounded the tiniest bit appealing, probably just for the chance to argue with her.

"She wants you to give me your nanny job, which you and I both know is ridiculous."

Oh, the *job*. Heat rose to the back of Sam's neck as he realized he'd misinterpreted his sister's actions as dating-type matchmaking. And, yes, it was ridiculous from his own point of view to hire someone as mouthy and inappropriate as Susan, but why did *she* find the idea ridiculous?

"Hi, Miss Hayashi," Mindy said, looking up at Susan with a shy smile.

"Hi, Mindy." Susan's voice went rich and warm as honey when she looked down at his daughter. "Want to come in and play with the dogs?"

"No, she can't come in!" The words practically exploded out of Sam's mouth.

"Oh." Susan looked surprised, and Mindy opened her mouth to object.

"She can't…" He nodded down at her. "It's not safe."

Xavier provided an unexpected escape route. "You're too little to come in here," he explained. "But I can take you to the barn and show you our new tiny puppies. There's eight of them, and they're all gray 'cept for one spotted one, and their eyes are shut like this!" He squeezed his eyes tightly shut, them immediately opened them, grinning.

"I want to see them!" Mindy jumped to her feet, hugged Sam's leg and gazed up at him. "Please, Daddy?"

Love for his daughter overwhelmed him. "Okay, if you have an adult with you."

Xavier ran a few yards down to the gate, and with an assist from Susan, got it open. "Come on, Dad will help us," he said, and the two children rushed off toward the barn.

Leaving Sam and Susan standing with a fence between them. "You shouldn't have invited Mindy to come in without my permission," he informed her.

"Right. You're right. I just…who knew you were *that* overprotective? She's not made of glass, but you're going to have her thinking she is."

"I think we've already established that you don't have the right to judge."

"Yeah, but that was when I was trying to get the job with you. Now, I'm just a…well, an acquaintance. Which means I can state my opinion, right?"

"She's an acquaintance with a double certification in elementary and special ed," his sister, Daisy, said, coming from behind to put a hand on Susan's shoulder. "Sam, when are you going to realize you're way too cautious with that child? Marie was even worse. You're going to have Mindy afraid of her own shadow."

"That day is a long way off," Sam said, frowning at the idea that Marie had been anything but the perfect mother. Did everyone think he was too overprotective? Was he? Was he hurting Mindy?

"Um, think I'll go help get the kids ready to go home." Susan walked off, shoulders squared and back straight.

Daisy glared up at Sam. "What's your problem, anyway? Susan said her interview with you didn't go well."

"Did she tell you she couldn't stop questioning my abilities as a father? I hardly think that's what I want in a summer nanny."

"Come on, let's walk up to the house," Daisy said, coming out through the gate and putting an arm around him. "Sam, everyone knows you're the best dad around. You stepped in when Marie got sick and you haven't taken a break since. If you're a tiny bit controlling, well, who can blame you? Mindy's not had an easy road."

"You're using your social worker voice, and I'm sensing a 'but' in there." He put his own arm around his little sister. She definitely drove him crazy, but he didn't question her wisdom. Daisy was the intuitive, people-smart one in the family, and Sam and his brother had learned early on to respect that.

"The thing is, you're looking for a clone of your dead wife. In a nanny and in a partner. What if you opened your mind to a different kind of influence on Mindy?"

"What do you mean, in a partner?" He'd kept his deathbed promise to Marie a secret, so how did Daisy know he was looking for a new mom for Mindy?

Daisy laughed. "I've seen the women you date. They're all chubby and blonde and worshipful. It's not rocket science to figure out that you're trying to find a replica of Marie."

The words stung with their truth. "Is that so bad? Marie was wonderful. We were happy." He'd never been like Daisy and Troy, adventurous and fun-loving; he'd always been the conventional older brother, wanting a standard, solid, traditional family life, and Marie had understood that. She'd wanted the same thing, and they'd been building it. Building a beautiful life that had been cut short.

"Oh, Sam." Daisy rubbed a hand up and down his back. "It's understandable. It was a horrible loss for you and Mindy. For all of us, really. I loved Marie, too."

Reassured, Sam could focus on the rest of what Daisy had said. "You think I need to be worshipped?"

"I think you're uncomfortable when women question your views, but c'mon, Sam. You're Mensa-level smart, you're practically a billionaire and you've built Hinton Enterprises into the most successful corporation in Rescue River, if not all of Ohio. It's not like you need reassurance about your masculinity. Why don't you try dating women who pose a little bit of a challenge?"

"I get plenty of challenge from my family, primarily you." He squeezed her shoulders, trying not to get defensive about her words. "My immediate problem is finding a nanny, not a girlfriend. And someone like Susan has values too different from mine. She'd have Mindy taming pit bulls and playing with hoodlums."

"She'd let Mindy out of the glass bubble you've put her in!" Daisy spun away to glare at him. "Look, she's the one with coursework in special ed, not you. She's not going to put your daughter at risk. She'd be great for Mindy, even if she does make you a little uncomfortable. And you did kind of contribute indirectly to her getting fired from her waitressing job."

A hard lump of guilt settled in his stomach. He didn't want to be the cause of someone losing their livelihood. He'd always prided himself on finding ways to keep from laying off employees, even in this tough economy.

She raised her eyebrows. "Think about it, bro. Are you man enough to handle a nanny like Susan, if it would be the best thing for Mindy?"

Susan sat at the kitchen table with Angelica and the new baby while Daisy warmed up the side dishes she'd brought and ordered her brothers outside to grill burgers.

"Do you want to hold her?" Angelica asked, looking down at the dark-haired baby as if she'd rather do anything than let her go.

"Me?" Susan squeaked. "No thanks. I mean, she's beautiful, but I'm a disaster with babies. At a minimum, I always make them cry."

Of course, Sam came back into the kitchen in time to hear that remark. She seemed to have a genius for *not* impressing him.

"I used to feel that way, too," Daisy said, "but I'm great with little Emmie. Here, you can stir this while I hold her." She put down her spoon and confidently scooped the baby out of Angelica's arms.

Susan walked over to the stove and looked doubtfully at the pan of something white and creamy. "You want me to help cook? Really?"

"Oh, never mind, I forgot. Sam, stir the white sauce for a minute, would you?"

"You don't cook?" he asked Susan as he took over at the stove, competently stirring with one hand while he reached for a pepper grinder with the other.

In for a penny, in for a pound. "Nope. Not domestic."

"You'll learn," Angelica said, stretching and

twisting her back. "When you find someone you want to cook for."

"Not happening. I'm the single type."

"She is," Daisy laughed. "She won't even date. But we're going to change all that."

"No, we're not." Susan sat back down at the table.

"Yes, we are. The group at church has big plans for you."

"*My* singles group? Who would run it if I somehow got involved with a guy?" Susan pulled her legs up and wrapped her arms around them, taking in the large, comfortable kitchen with appreciation. Old woodwork and gingham curtains blended with the latest appliances, and there was even a couch in the corner. Perfect.

She enjoyed Daisy and enjoyed being here with her family because she'd never had anything like this. Her family had been small and a little bit isolated, and while Donny was great in his way, you couldn't joke around with him.

She watched Sam stir the sauce, taste it, season it some more. This was another side of the impatient businessman. Really, was there anything the man wasn't good at?

He probably saw her as a bumbling incompetent. She couldn't succeed at waitressing, at cooking, at holding a baby. He thought she'd be bad for his daughter, that much had been obvious.

Too bad, because she needed the money, and Mindy was adorable. Kids were never the problem; it was the adults who always did her in.

Suddenly, the door burst open and Xavier rushed through, followed closely by Mindy. "Give it back. Give it back!" she was yelling as she grabbed at something in his hands.

"No, Mindy, it's mine!"

Mindy stopped, saw all the adults staring at her, and threw herself to the floor, holding her breath, legs kicking.

Sam dropped the spoon with a clatter and went to her side. "Mindy, Mindy honey, it's okay."

The child ignored him, lost in her own rapidly escalating emotional reaction.

"Mindy!" He scolded her. "Sit up right now." He tried to urge her into an upright position, but she went as rigid as a board, her ear-splitting screams making everyone cringe.

Sam was focused on her with love and concern, but at this point that wasn't enough. Susan knew that interfering wasn't wise, but for better or worse, she had a gift. She understood special-needs kids, and she had a hunch she could calm Mindy down.

She sank to her knees beside the pair. "Shhhh," she whispered ever so softly into Mindy's ear. "Shhhh." Gently, she slid closer in behind the little girl and raised her eyebrows at Sam, tacitly asking permission.

He shrugged, giving it.

She wrapped her arms around Mindy from behind, whispering soothing sounds into her ear, sounds without words. Sounds that always soothed Donny, actually. She rubbed one hand up and down Mindy's arm, gently coercing her to be calm. While she wasn't a strict proponent of holding therapy, she knew that sometimes physical contact worked when nothing else could reach a kid.

"Leave me 'lone!" Mindy cried with a little further struggle, but Susan just kept up her gentle hold and her wordless sounds, and Mindy slowly relaxed.

"He has a picture frame that says…" She drew in a gasping breath. "It says, Mom. *M-O-M*, Mom. I want it!"

Sam went pale, and Susan's heart ached with sympathy for the pair. Losing a parent was about the worst thing that could happen to a kid. And losing a wife was horrible, but it had to be even more painful to watch your child suffer and not know how to help.

To his credit, Sam regrouped quickly. "Honey, you can't take Xavier's picture frame. But we can get you one, okay?"

"It might even be fun to make one yourself," Susan suggested, paying attention to the way the child's body relaxed at the sound of her father's reassuring words. "Then it would be even more special. Do you have lots of pictures of your mom?"

"Yes, 'cause I'm afraid I'll forget her and then she'll never come back."

Perfectly normal for a five-year-old to think her dead mother would come back. But ouch. Poor Mindy, poor Sam. She hugged the child a little tighter.

"Hon, Mommy's not coming back, remember? She's with Jesus." Sam's tone changed enough on the last couple of words that Susan guessed he might have his doubts about that. Doubts he wasn't conveying to Mindy, of course.

"But if I'm really good…"

"No, sweetie." Sam's face looked gray with sadness. "Mommy can't come back to this world, but we'll see her in heaven."

"I don't like that!" Mindy's voice rose to a roar. "I. Don't. Like. That!"

"None of us do, honey." Daisy squatted before her, patting the sobbing child's arm, her forehead wrinkling. "I don't know what to do when she's like this," she said quietly to Susan.

"Mommy!" Mindy wailed over and over. "I'll be good," she added in a gulp.

Sam and Daisy looked helplessly at each other over Mindy's head.

"It's not your fault. You're a good, good girl. Mommy loved you." Susan kept her arms wrapped tightly around Mindy and rocked, whispering and humming a wordless song. Every so often Mindy would tense up again, and Susan whispered the soothing words. "Not your fault. Mommy loved you, and Daddy loves you."

She knew the words were true, even though she hadn't known Sam and his wife as a family. And she knew that Mindy needed to hear it, over and over again.

She was glad to be here. Glad she had enough distance to help Sam with what was a very tough situation.

Very slowly, Mindy started to relax again. Daisy shot Susan a smile and moved away to check the stove.

"Shhh, shhh," Susan whispered, still holding her, still rocking. Losing a piece of her heart to this sweet, angry, hurting child.

Finally, Mindy went limp, and Susan very carefully slid her over to Sam. Took a deep breath, and tried to emerge from her personal, very emotional reaction and get back to the professional. "Does she usually fall asleep after a meltdown?"

Sam nodded. "Wears herself out, poor kid." He stroked her hair, whispering the same kind of sounds Susan had made, and Mindy's eyes closed.

"She'll need something to eat and drink soon, maybe some chocolate milk, something like that," Susan said quietly after a couple of minutes. "Protein and carbs."

"Thank you for calming her down," he said, his voice quiet, too. "That was much shorter than she usually goes."

"No problem, it's kind of my job. Did she have tantrums before you lost your wife?"

Sam nodded. "She's always been volatile. We thought it was because of her hand."

Susan reached out and stroked Mindy's blond hair, listening to the welcome sound of the child's sleep-breathing. "Having a disability can be frustrating. Or she could have some other sensitivities. Some kids are just more reactive."

"Did you learn how to be a child-whisperer in your special ed training?"

Susan chuckled. "Some, but mostly, you learn it when you have a brother with autism. Donny—that's my little brother—used to have twenty tantrums per day. It was too much for my mom, so I helped take care of him."

Sam's head lifted. "Where's Donny now?"

"Home with Mom in California," she said. "He's eighteen, and…" She broke off. He was eighteen, and still expecting to be going to a camp focused on his beloved birds and woodland animals, because she hadn't had the heart to call and tell him she'd screwed up and there wasn't any money. "He's still a handful, that's for sure, but he's also a joy."

Mindy burrowed against her father's chest, whimpering a little.

"How long has it been since you lost your wife?" Susan asked quietly.

"Two years, and Mindy does fine a lot of the time. And then we have this." He nodded down at her.

"Grief is funny that way." Susan searched her mind for her coursework on it. "From what I've read, she might re-grieve at each developmental stage. If she was pre-operational when your wife died, she didn't fully understand it. Could be that now, she's starting to take in the permanence of the loss."

"I just want to fix it." Sam's voice was grim. "She doesn't deserve this pain."

"No one deserves it, but it happens." She put a hand over Sam's. "I'm sorry for your loss. And sorry this is so hard on Mindy, too. You're doing a good job."

"Coming from you, that means something," he said with a faint grin.

Their eyes caught for a second too long.

Then Angelica and Daisy came bustling back into the room—when had they left, anyway?—followed by Xavier. How long had she, Sam and Mindy been sitting in the middle of the kitchen floor?

"Hey, the potatoes are done," Daisy said, expertly pouring the contents of one pan into another. She leaned over and called out through the open window. "Troy, how about those burgers?"

"They're ready." Troy came in with a plate stacked high with hamburgers, plus a few hot dogs on the side.

Sam moved to the couch at the side of the kitchen, cuddling a half-asleep Mindy, while the rest of them hustled to get food on the table. Susan folded napkins and carried dishes and generally felt a part of things, which was nice. She hadn't felt this comfortable in a long time. Being around Mindy, she felt as if she was in her element. This was her craft. What she was good at.

Again, she couldn't help comparing this evening to those she'd spent with her own family. The tension between her mom and dad, the challenges Donny presented, made family dinners stressful, and as often as not, the kids had eaten separately from the adults, watching TV. Susan could see the appeal of this lifestyle, living near your siblings, getting to know their kids. Cousins growing up together.

This was what she'd want for her own kid.

And where on earth had that thought come from? She totally didn't want kids! And she didn't want a husband. She was a career girl, and that was that.

So why did she feel so strangely at home here?

Chapter Three

A while after dinner, Sam came back into the kitchen after settling Mindy and Xavier in the den with a movie.

The room felt empty. "Where's Susan?"

"She left." Daisy looked up from her phone. "Said something about packing."

"She's going on a trip?" That figured. She seemed like a world traveler, much too sophisticated to spend her free summer in their small town. Applying for the job as Mindy's nanny had probably been just a whim.

Then again, she'd mentioned needing to help support her mother and brother…

And why he was so interested in figuring out her motives and whereabouts, he didn't have a clue.

"No…" Daisy was back to texting, barely

paying attention. "She's gotta move back home for the summer."

"Move?"

"Yeah, to California."

"What? Why?"

Daisy was too engrossed in her phone to answer, and following a sudden urge, Sam turned and walked out into the warm evening. He caught up to Susan just as she opened her car door. "Weren't you even going to say goodbye?"

"Did I hurt your feelings?" she asked lightly, turning back to him, looking up.

She was so beautiful it made him lose his breath. So he just stared down at her.

It must be the way she'd helped Mindy that had changed her in his eyes, softened her sharp edges, made her not just cute but deeply appealing.

And he obviously needed to get on with his dating project, because he was having a serious overreaction to Susan. "Daisy said you're leaving town."

She wrinkled her nose. "Yeah, in a few days. Got to go back to California for the summer."

"You're not driving that, are you?" Lightly, he kicked the tire of her rusty subcompact.

"No! I'm taking the Mercedes." She chuckled, a deep, husky sound at odds with her petite frame. "Of course I'm driving this, Sam. It's my car."

"It's not safe."

She just raised her eyebrows at him. As if to ask what right he had to make such a comment. And it was a good question: What right *did* he have?

The moonlight spilled down on them and the sky was a black velvet canopy sprinkled with millions of diamond stars. He cleared his throat. "Does this mean you don't want the job?"

"Does this mean I'm still in the running?" There was a slightly breathy sound to her voice.

They were standing close together.

"You are," he said slowly. "I liked… No. I was amazed at how you were able to calm Mindy." He couldn't stop looking at her.

She stepped backward and gave an awkward smile. "Years of experience with my brother. And the coursework. All the grief stuff. You could call a local college, find someone with similar qualifications."

"I doubt that. I'd like to hire you."

"We don't get along. I wouldn't be good at this. I mean, nannying? Living in? Seriously, ask anyone, I'm not cut out for family life."

He cocked his head to one side, wondering suddenly about her past. "Oh?"

She waved her hand rapidly. "I was engaged once. It…didn't work out."

He nodded, inexplicably relieved. "Maybe you should come work for me on a trial basis, then."

"A…trial basis?" That breathy sound again.

"Yes, since you're not cut out for family life. It's a live-in job, after all."

"I do need a place to stay," she said, "but no. That wouldn't look right, would it? Me living in your house."

Her eyes were wide and suddenly, Sam felt an urge to protect her. "Of course, I wouldn't want to compromise your reputation. We have a mother-in-law's suite over the garage. It has a separate entrance and plenty of privacy."

"Really? You're offering me the job? Because remember, I can't cook."

"You can learn."

"Maybe, maybe not. I… What made you change your mind? I thought you didn't like me." She was nibbling on her lower lip, and right now she looked miles from the confident, brash waitress who'd stood up to a business-man in front of a restaurant full of people.

He smiled down at her. "My sister. My brother. And the way you handled Mindy."

"But she's probably not going to have another trauma reaction for a long time. Whereas cooking's every day. You really don't want to hire me."

"Why are you trying to talk me out of it?" Her resistance was lighting a fire in him, making him feel as if he had to have her, and only her, for Mindy's nanny. "I do want to. The sooner the better. When could you start?"

"Well…" She was starting to cave, and triumph surged through him. "My room is going to be remodeled out from under me starting this weekend."

"Great," he said, leaning in to close the deal. "I'll have a truck sent round tomorrow. You can start setting up your apartment over the garage."

"You're sure?"

"I'm sure."

"Paying what you told me before?"

He flashed a wide smile. "Of course."

She paused, her nose wrinkling. Looked up at the stars. Then a happy expression broke out on her face. "Thank you!" she said, and gave him a quick, firm handshake.

Her smile and her touch sent a shot of joy

through his entire body. He hadn't felt anything like that before, ever. Not even when Marie was alive.

Guilt overwhelmed him and he took a step back. "Remember, it's just a trial," he said.

What had he gotten himself into?

Of course, everyone and his brother was in downtown Rescue River the next Saturday morning to comment on the moving truck in front of Susan's boarding house. The truck carrying Susan to her absolute doom, if the scuttlebutt was to be believed.

"So you're the next victim," said Miss Minnie Falcon, who'd hurried over from the Senior Towers, pushing her wheeled walker, to watch the moving activities. "Sam Hinton eats babysitters for lunch!"

"It's just on a trial basis," Susan said, pausing in front of the guesthouse's front porch. "If I don't like the job, I can leave at any time. Don't you want to sit down, Miss Minnie?"

"Oh, no, I'd rather stand," the gray-haired woman said, her eyes bright. "Don't want to miss anything!"

"Okay, if you're sure." That was small-town life: your activities were like reality TV to your neighbors, and truthfully, Susan found it sweet. At least everyone knew who you were and watched out for you.

"I'm going to miss you so much," her landlady, Lacey, said as she helped Susan carry her sole box of fragile items down the rickety porch steps. "I'm really sorry about making you move. It's just that Buck seems to be serious about staying sober, and he's looking to make money, and of course, he's willing to work on this place for cheap because he's my brother."

"It's fine. You've got to remodel while you can," Susan soothed her. "And we'll still hang out, right?" She'd enjoyed her year at Lacey's guesthouse, right in the heart of her adopted town. She wouldn't have minded staying. But sometimes, she felt silly being twenty-five years old and having to use someone else's kitchen if she wanted to make herself a snack.

"Of course we'll hang out. I'll miss you!"

"I know, me, too." She and Lacey had gotten close during a number of late-night talks. Susan had comforted Lacey through a heartbreaking miscarriage, and they'd cried and prayed together.

"And it's not just me. The cats will miss you!" Lacey said. "You have to come back and visit all the time."

As if to prove her words, an ancient gray cat tangled himself around Susan's ankle and then, when she grabbed the bannister to keep from tripping, offered up a mournful yowl.

Susan reached down to rub the old tomcat's head. "You and Mrs. Whiskers take care of yourselves. I'll bring you a treat when I come back, promise."

They went outside and loaded the box of breakables into the front seat of Susan's car, only to be accosted by Gramps Camden, another resident of the Senior Towers. "Old Sam Hinton caught himself a live one!" he said. "Now you listen here. Those Hintons are trouble. Just because my granddaughter married one—and Troy is the best of the bunch—that doesn't mean they're a good family. I was cheated by that schemer's dad and now, his corporation won't let up on me about selling my farm. You be careful in his house. Lock your door!"

"I will." She'd gotten to know Gramps through the schools, where he now served as a volunteer.

"He wasn't good enough for that wife of his," Gramps continued.

"Marie was pretty nearly perfect," agreed Miss Minnie Falcon.

From what Susan already knew about Sam, she figured any woman who married him would have to be. And yet, for all his millionaire arrogance, he obviously adored his little daughter. And a man who loved a child that much couldn't be all bad. Could he?

"Is that all your stuff, ma'am?" the college-age guy, who'd apparently come with the truck, asked respectfully.

Gramps waved and headed back to the Towers with Miss Minnie.

"Yes, that's it," Susan said. "What do I owe you?"

"Nothing. Mr. Hinton took care of it."

"Let me grab my purse. I want to at least give you a tip for being so careful."

The young man waved his hand. "Mr. Hinton took care of that, too. He said we weren't to take a penny from you."

"Is that so," Susan said, torn between gratitude and irritation.

"Money's one thing Sam Hinton doesn't lack." The voice belonged to Buck Armstrong, Lacey's brother. He put a large potted plant into the back of her car, tilting it sideways so it would fit. The young veteran had haunted eyes and a bad reputation, but whenever Susan had run into him visiting his sister, he'd been nothing but a gentleman. "You all set?"

"I hope so. I'm hearing horror stories about my new boss, is all." And they were spooking her. As the time came to leave her friendly guesthouse in the heart of Rescue River, she felt more and more nervous.

Buck nodded, his eyes darkening. "Sam didn't use to be quite so…driven. Losing a wife is hard on a guy."

Sympathy twisted Susan's heart. Buck knew what he was talking about; he'd lost not only his wife, but their baby as well. That was what had pushed him toward drinking too much, according to Lacey.

"You giving this gal a hard time?" The voice belonged to Rescue River's tall, dark-skinned police chief. He clapped Buck on the shoulder in a friendly way, but his eyes were watchful. Chief Dion Coleman had probably had a number of encounters with Buck that weren't so friendly.

"He's trying to tell me Sam Hinton is really a nice guy, since I'm going to work for him," Susan explained.

Dion let out a hearty laugh. "You're going to work for Sam? Doing what?"

"Summer nanny for Mindy."

"Is that right? My, my." Dion shook his head, still chuckling. "I tell you what, I think Mr. Sam Hinton might have finally met his match."

"What's that supposed to mean?" Susan asked, indignant.

"Nothing, nothing." He clapped Buck's shoulder again. "Come on, man, I'll buy you a cup of coffee if you've got half an hour to spare. Got something to run by you."

Buck was about to get gently evangelized, if Susan knew Dion. He headed up a men's prayer group at their church and was unstoppable in his efforts to get the hurting men of Rescue River on the right path. According to Daisy, he'd done wonders with her brother Troy.

As Buck and Dion headed toward the Chatterbox Café, Lacey came out to hug her goodbye. "You'll be fine. This is going to be an adventure!" She lowered her voice. "At least, let's hope so."

An odd, uncomfortable chill tickled Susan's spine as she climbed into her car and headed to her new job, her new life.

Chapter Four

Sam paced back and forth in the driveway, checking his watch periodically. Where was she?

Small beach shoes clacked along the walkway from the back deck, and he turned around just in time to catch Mindy in his arms. He lifted her and gave her a loud kiss on the cheek, making her giggle.

And then she struggled down. "Daddy, Miss Lou Ann says I can play in the pool if it's okay with you. Can I?"

Lou Ann Miller, who'd worked for his family back in the day and had helped to raise Sam, Troy and Daisy, followed her young charge out into the driveway. "She's very excited. It would be a nice way for her to cool off." She winked at him. "Nice for you if she'd burn off some extra energy, too."

Sam hesitated. Lou Ann was an amazing woman, but she was in her upper seventies. "If she stays in the shallow end," he decided. "And Mindy, you listen to Miss Lou Ann."

"Of course she will," Lou Ann said. "Run and change into your suit, sweetie." As soon as Mindy disappeared inside, Lou Ann put a hand on her hip and raised an eyebrow at Sam. "I was the county synchronized swimming champion eight years running," she said. "And I still swim every morning. I can get Mindy out of any trouble she might get into."

"Of course!" Sam felt himself reddening and reminded himself not to stereotype.

He just wanted to keep Mindy safe and get her home environment as close to what Marie had made as was humanly possible. Get things at home back to running like a well-organized company, one he could lead with confidence and authority.

The moving truck chugged around the corner and up to the house, and Sam rubbed his hands together. Here was one step…he hoped. If Susan worked out.

He gestured them toward the easiest unloading point and helped open the back of the truck as Susan pulled up in her old subcompact, its slightly-too-dark exhaust and more-than-slightly-too-loud engine announcing that the car was on its last legs. He'd have to do something about that.

As the college boys he'd hired started moving her few possessions out, she approached. Her clothes were relaxed—a loose gauzy shirt, flip flops and cut-off shorts revealing long, slender, golden-bronzed legs—but her face looked pinched with stress. "Hey," she said, following his glance back to her car. "Don't worry, I'll pull it behind the garage as soon as the truck's out of the way."

"I didn't say—"

"You didn't have to." She grabbed a box off the truck and headed up the stairs.

He helped the guys unload a heavy, overstuffed chair and then followed them up the stairs with an armload of boxes.

There was Susan, staring around the apartment, hands on hips.

"What's wrong?" he asked. "Is it suitable? Too small? We can work something out—"

"It's fine," she said, patting his arm. "It's beautiful. I'm just trying to decide where to put things."

"Good." There was something about Susan that seemed a little volatile, as if she might morph into a butterfly and disappear. "Well, you need to put the desk in that corner," he said, gesturing the movers to the part of the living room that was alcoved off, "and the armchair over there."

"Wait. Put the desk under the window. I like to look out while I work."

The young guys looked at him, tacitly asking his permission.

Susan raised her eyebrows, looking from the movers to Sam. There was another moment of silence.

"Of course, of course! Whatever the lady wants." But when they got the desk, a crooked and ill-finished thing, into the light under the window, he frowned. "I might have an extra desk you can use, if you like."

"I'm fine with that one."

He understood pride, but he hated to see a teacher with such a ratty desk. "Really?"

"Yes." She waited while the young movers went down to get another load, then spun on him. "Don't you have something else to do, other than comment about my stuff?"

"I'm sorry." He was controlling and he knew it, but it was with the goal of making other people's lives better. "I just thought…are you sure you wouldn't rather have something less…lopsided? The money's not a problem."

She walked to the desk and ran a hand over it, smiling when one finger encountered a dipped spot. "My brother made it for me at his vocational school," she explained. "It was his graduation project, and he kept it a secret. When he gave it to me, it was about the best moment of my life."

"Oh." Sam felt like a heel. "So he's a woodworker?"

She shook her head. "No, not really. He's still finding his way, but the fact that he pushed past the frustration and made something so big, mostly by himself…and that he did it for me…it means a lot, that's all." She cleared her throat and got very busy flicking dust off an immaculate built-in shelf as the college boys came in with another load.

Obviously her brother was important to her. And obviously, Sam needed to pay attention to something other than just the monetary value of things.

He didn't have any family furniture, heirloom or sentimental or otherwise. For one thing, his dad still had most of their old stuff out at the family estate. For another, Marie had liked everything new, and he'd enjoyed providing it for her.

As the movers carried the last load into the bedroom, Susan looked up at him, then rose gracefully to her feet. "I was going to spend a little time getting settled. But is there something I can do for you and Mindy first?"

"Do you need help unpacking?"

One corner of her mouth quirked up, and he got the uncomfortable feeling she was laughing at him. "No, Sam," she said, her voice almost...gentle. "I've moved probably five or six times since college. I'm pretty good at it."

Of course she had, and the fact that she looked so young—and had a vulnerable side— didn't mean he had to take care of her. She was an employee with a job to do. "I'll be in the house," he said abruptly. "Come in as soon as you're set up, and we'll discuss your duties."

As he left, he saw one of the college boys give Susan a sympathetic glance.

What was that all about? He just wanted to have things settled as soon as possible. Was that so wrong?

Okay, maybe he was pushing her a little bit, but that was what you did with new employees: you let them know how things were going to be, what the rules were. This was, for all intents and purposes, an orientation, and he wanted to make sure to do things right.

But he guessed he didn't need to rearrange her furniture. And given her reaction to the desk suggestion, she probably wouldn't welcome his getting his car dealer to find her a better car, either.

No, Susan seemed independent. Which was great, but also worrisome. He wondered how well she would fit in with his plan for a traditional, family-oriented summer for Mindy. What changes would she want to make?

He walked by the pool and saw with relief that Mindy was happily occupied with her inflatable shark in the shallow end.

Lou Ann Miller sat at the table in the shade. He did a double take. Was that a magazine she was reading? He opened his mouth to remind her that Mindy needed close attention. When Marie had brought Mindy out to the pool, before she'd gotten too sick to do it, she'd been right there in the water with her.

But the moment Mindy ventured away from the edge of the pool, LouAnn pushed herself to her feet and walked over to stand nearby.

"See what I can do!" Mindy crowed as she swam a little, her stroke awkward. She had an adaptive flotation device for her arm, but she didn't like to use it.

"Try kicking more with your feet, honey," LouAnn said. "If you get tired, you can flip over to your back."

"Show me how?"

"Sure." Lou Ann shrugged out of her terry-cloth cover-up, tossed it back toward the table and walked down the steps into the water, barely touching the railing. She wore a violet tank suit and her short hair didn't seem to require a swim cap.

Glad he hadn't interfered and satisfied with Lou Ann's abilities as a caregiver and swim instructor, Sam strode toward the house. He hoped Susan wouldn't take long to get settled and come down. The sooner they established her duties, the sooner things could go back to normal.

He'd just finished a sandwich when there was a tap on the back door.

"You ready for me?" Susan asked, poking her head inside. "Am I supposed to knock or just come in? I really don't know how to be a nanny."

"Just come in." If he needed privacy, there was the whole upstairs. "I'm ready. Let me give you a quick tour so you know where things are."

"Great." She was looking around the kitchen. "Is this where you spend most of your time?"

He nodded. "It's a mess. Sorry. My cleaning people come on Mondays."

"You call this a mess?" She laughed. "I can barely tell you have a kid."

"Mindy's pretty neat. Me, I have to restrain my inner slob. Plus, Lou Ann Miller's been helping me until I find…well, until I found you. She's a whiz at cooking and cleaning."

"Why didn't you just hire her?" Susan asked as he led her into the living room.

"She doesn't want a permanent job. Says she's too old, though I don't see much evidence of her slowing down. This is where we…where I…well, where we used to entertain a lot." The room had been Marie's pride and joy, but Sam and Mindy didn't use it much, and he realized that, without a party full of people in it, the place looked like a museum.

Susan didn't comment on the living room nor the dining room with its polished cherry table and Queen Anne chairs. He swept her past the closed-off sunroom, of course. When they got to Mindy's playroom, Susan perked up. "This is nice!"

She walked over to inspect the play kitchen and peeked into the dollhouse. "What wonderful toys," she said almost wistfully. She looked at the easel and smiled approvingly at the train set. "Good, you're not being sexist. I see you got her some cars, too."

"Those are partly for my sake," he admitted. "I go nuts after too many games with dolls."

"Me, too." She walked over to perch on the window seat, crossing her arms as she surveyed the playroom. "It's a big place for one little girl."

A familiar ache squeezed Sam's chest. "We were going to fill it up with kids." He stared out the window and down the green lawn. "But plans don't always work out."

When he looked back at her, she was watching him with a thoughtful expression on her face. "That must be hard to deal with."

He acknowledged the sympathy with a nod. "We're managing."

"Do you ever think of moving?"

"No!" In truth, he had. He'd longed to move, but it wouldn't be fair to Marie's memory. She'd wanted him to continue on as they'd begun, to create the life they'd imagined together for Mindy. "We're fine here," he said firmly.

She arched one delicate brow. "Well, okay

then." She stood up, looked around and gave a decisive nod. "I know a lot of kids, so we'll work on filling up the playroom and pool with them this summer. This place is crying out for noise and fun."

"Vetted by me," he warned. "I don't want a lot of kids I don't know coming over."

"You want to approve every playdate?"

"For now, yes."

She pressed her lips together, obviously trying not to smile, but a dimple showed on her face. A very cute dimple.

"Hey, look. I'm a control freak, especially where Mindy is concerned."

"No kidding." She raised her eyebrows in mock surprise. "It's okay, Sam. We'll figure out a way to manage this. But Mindy does need friends around this summer. She needs to work on her social skills."

"There's nothing wrong—"

She cocked her head to one side and tucked her chin and looked at him.

"Her social skills are okay." He frowned at Susan's pointed silence. "Aren't they?"

"It's not a big problem," Susan said. "But she's very sensitive about her disability and her mother, or lack of one. I've broken up several playground brawls. The best way to work on it is to give her lots of free-play experience with other kids." She squatted down beside the bookshelves that lined one side of the room. "And there are books that can help. But these—" She ran a delicate finger along the spines of the books. "These are books for toddlers, Sam. She can read better than this."

Her criticism stung, but he nodded. "Her mother was the big book-buyer. That's why I'm glad you're here, Susan. I can see that you have an expertise the other candidates didn't have. I want to do right by Mindy."

"Weekly trips to the library. Fern can help us pick out some good books, including ones about social skills."

"Sure." He led the way back through the kitchen. "Now, I don't expect you to cook for us—"

"That's good," she interrupted. "Remember, I'm a disaster in the kitchen."

"I'm sure you can figure out how to make breakfast and lunch. I'll do dinner, or order it in. But I do want you to eat dinner with us most nights."

"What?" She froze, staring at him.

"It's better for Mindy," he explained. "All kinds of studies show the importance of family dinners. I'd like to have you be a part of that."

She looked a little trapped. "I'm not your family, I'm a hired—"

"Five days per week," he bargained. "You can have a couple of nights off."

Through the open kitchen window, he could hear Lou Ann and Mindy laughing together in the backyard. He leaned back against the granite counter and watched an array of expressions cross Susan's face.

Was he being unfair, demanding too much of her? He'd looked over lists of nanny duties online, and while having a sitter eat with the family wasn't common, he'd seen a few examples of it being done. He was paying her well, much better than the average.

"You have to eat," he reminded her. "It's free food."

She chuckled, a throaty sound that made all his senses spring to life. "We'll give it a try."

He pushed his advantage. "And Sunday dinner is the most important meal of all, so I'd appreciate your being there. I think we agreed that you'd work Sunday afternoons and take a weekday afternoon off, correct?"

"You mean, like, tomorrow?"

He nodded. Best to start out as you meant to go on. "Yes. Definitely tomorrow."

"We'll give it a try," she repeated doubtfully. "But I'm not…well. We'll see."

Score one for him. But her resistance proved this wasn't going to be as easy as he'd hoped.

The next day, Susan stood at the kitchen counter scooping deli salads into bowls. Even though she'd turned down Sam's offer of an apron to protect her church clothes—which, hello, consisted of a faded denim skirt with a lime-green tee and sneakers, hardly designer duds that needed special care—she still felt uncomfortable and out of place. She was used to grabbing a bagel with friends or fixing herself a peanut butter sandwich after church. Fixing a family lunch in a big, fancy kitchen was way out of her comfort zone.

Since she attended the same church as Sam and Mindy, it had made sense to all go together. Uncomfortable with the intimacy of that, she'd made a beeline for her singles group friends once they'd gotten there, but she hadn't had a choice about a ride home, which had included a stop at the grocery store for supplies.

It was all too, too domestic. And Sam had been entirely too appealing during the grocery story visit, brawny arms straining his golf shirt, thoughtfully discussing salad options with the deli clerk, whose name he remembered and whose children he asked about.

And since Sunday dinner was, quote, the most important meal of the week, here she was helping to cook it, or at least dish it up. Though she didn't see the point of setting the table and putting deli food into serving dishes when all Mindy wanted was to play in the pool.

Through the window, she studied Sam and Mindy, side by side on the deck while Sam grilled chicken. He was talking seriously to her, explaining the knobs on the gas grill and putting out a restrictive arm when she came too close.

Sam. What a character. He might be the head of an empire, able to boss around his employees and make each day go according to plan, but he wasn't going to be able to control everything that happened in his own home. Not with a kid. Kids were never predictable.

And he couldn't control her, either. She had to maintain some sense of independence or the cage door would shut on her, just as it had almost done with her former fiancé. Encouraged by her father, they'd gotten engaged too quickly, before they knew each other well. Once Frank had found out what she was really like, he hadn't wanted her. And she'd been guiltily, giddily happy to get free.

She wasn't the marrying kind. And this stint in a housewifely role was temporary, just long enough to help her family financially.

From the front of the house, she heard a female voice. "Yoo-hoo! Surprise!"

Susan spun toward the sound, accidentally flinging a spoonful of macaroni salad on the floor in the process. "In here," she called. Then she grabbed a paper towel to clean up the dabs of macaroni scattered across the floor.

"Who are *you*?" asked a voice above her.

"It must be some of the hired help, Mama," said a male voice.

Susan paused in her wiping and looked up to see a yacht-club-looking, silver-haired couple. She gave the floor a last swipe, rinsed her hands and then turned to face them as she dried her hands on the dishtowel. "Hi, I'm Susan. Mindy's summer nanny. Who are you?" She softened the question with a smile.

"I didn't know he was hiring someone," the woman said, frowning. "He should have asked me. I know several nice young women who could have helped out."

"Now, Mama, maybe there's a reason he wanted to do things his own way." The man looked meaningfully at Susan. "We're Mindy's grandparents," he explained. "We like to pop in when we can on Sundays."

"That macaroni salad is from Shop Giant?" the woman asked, picking up the container and studying it. Then she walked over to the refrigerator, opened it, and scanned the contents.

Susan took a breath. There was no reason to feel defensive of this kitchen; it wasn't hers. "Yes, Sam picked it up on the way home from church."

"Oh, men." The woman waved a perfectly manicured hand. "They never know what to get, and with Sam so busy... Are you in charge of the cooking? Because I'd recommend Denise's Deli in town, if you don't have time to make homemade."

Susan's stomach knotted and she flashed back to her mom trying to please her dad with her culinary skills. It was a role Susan had vowed to avoid, so why was she feeling as if she needed to make an excuse for not having labored over doing all the chopping and boiling herself? For a family that, after all, wasn't her own?

The door from the deck burst open. "Grandma! Grandpa!" Mindy shrieked. She flung herself at the man.

He bent to pick her up. "Oh, missy, you're getting too heavy for an old man!"

Sam followed with a plate of grilled chicken breasts. "Hey, Ralph, Helen. I thought you two might stop by."

He had? Why hadn't he warned her?

"We can slide a couple of extra places in at the table. Susan, would you mind…"

"Consider it done," she said drily, adding just one place setting. And then, as soon as both grandparents were occupied with Mindy's excited explanation of the grilling process, she grabbed Sam's arm and pulled him into the playroom that adjoined the kitchen. "Look, since it's a family meal, I'm just going to leave you to it," she said. "Everything's ready to go here, and I've got a new thriller from the library that's calling my name."

"You have to eat," he said, frowning. "I'd like it if you'd stay."

"They seem a little…overwhelming," she admitted. "I'd feel more comfortable if—"

"Come on, Miss Susan, you forgot to make a place for Grandma! I got the extra placemats."

"Just stay for dinner," Sam said as Mindy tugged at her hand. "Then you can take off all afternoon."

"But—"

"I'm paying you to be here."

Clenching her teeth, Susan helped Mindy add another place setting to the table.

They all stood around it, and Sam said a prayer, and then they took their seats. Susan busied herself for a couple of minutes with bringing over food and fetching drinks, but then that was done and Sam urged her to sit down.

"Oh," the grandma, Helen, said, "are you eating with the family?"

Susan raised an eyebrow at Sam. "Not my idea."

"Susan's agreed to eat with us. Mindy needs a female role model."

"Oh, right," the older woman said. "At least until…" She gave Sam a meaningful look.

"Right," he said.

So was something in the works, then? Was Yacht Club Grandma cooking up a girlfriend for Sam? That would be ideal, Susan told herself as she helped cut Mindy's chicken breast. It would take her off the hot seat and out of a role she obviously wasn't suited for.

Amidst the clanking silverware and clinking glasses, there was a noticeable absence of small talk. Finally, the awkward silence was broken by Mindy's grandfather. "What *are* you?" he asked Susan.

"Hey, now, Ralph…" Sam started, a flush crossing his face.

Susan drew in her breath and let it out in a sigh. "It's fine," she said to Sam. She'd been answering that question all her life, but the questions had gotten a little more frequent since she'd moved from California to the Midwest.

Mindy looked alertly from one adult to the next, sensing the tension.

"I meant no offense," Ralph said, lifting both hands, palms up. "I'm just curious. You look a little…" He broke off, as if he was trying to think of the word.

As a person who blurted out the wrong thing herself fairly often, Susan thought it best to cut off his speculation. "I'm half-Japanese."

The older man snapped his fingers. "I thought so! You look a little bit Mexican, but I was guessing Oriental. Your mom's Japanese?"

Yes, he was a blurter. But that was so much more comfortable than his wife's sputtering disapproval. She smiled at him. "Nope. We don't fit the stereotype. It's my dad who's Japanese."

"Your English sounds just fine," the older man said reassuringly.

"I hope so!" Susan said, chuckling. "I was born in California."

Helen made a strangled sound in her throat, whether regarding California, Japan, or her husband's line of questioning, Susan wasn't sure.

"California," Mindy broke in, "that's where earthquakes are, and Hollywood."

"You're right!" Susan smiled at Mindy. Hooray for kids, who could break through adult tension with their innocent remarks. She took a bite of macaroni salad. Not bad. She'd definitely choose Shop Giant's brand over anything she could make herself.

"Mommy was from Ohio, like me," Mindy informed Susan. "You're sitting just where she used to sit."

Everyone froze.

Wow. Susan's stomach twisted. She hadn't meant to intrude, hadn't wanted to take anyone's place. Should she apologize? Offer to move? Ignore the remark? Suddenly, the food tasted as dry as ashes in her mouth.

"Mindy," Sam said, taking the child's hand in his own, "honey, saying that might make our guest feel uncomfortable."

He was right, it did…but that wasn't something Mindy should have to worry about. Just like that, Susan's own discomfort melted away as her training clicked in. Stifling a child's natural comments about a loss was a way to push grief underground, causing all sorts of psychological issues. "That's probably kind of sad for everybody," Susan said quickly. "Did your mom like to cook out?"

Mindy looked uncertainly at her father. "I think…she liked to lie down the best."

Susan's throat constricted. Mindy had only been four when her mom died. She couldn't remember much of what had happened when she was younger, of course.

Couldn't remember her mother as a healthy woman.

"Oh, no, Marie *loved* cooking of all kinds." Helen's eyes filled with tears. "You just don't remember, honey, because she was sick."

Ralph was staring down at his plate.

This wonderful family meal was turning into an outright disaster. The grief of parents who'd lost their beloved daughter was *way* beyond Susan's ability to soothe. She met Sam's gaze across the table. *Do something*, she tried to telegraph with her eyes.

Sam cleared his throat and brushed a hand

over Mindy's hair. "I remember how Mom loved to make cookies with you," he said. "At Christmastime, you two would get all set up with icing and sprinkles and colored sugar. Mom let you decorate the cookies however you wanted."

Susan breathed out a sigh of relief and smiled encouragingly at Sam. He was doing exactly the right thing. "That sounds like fun!"

"Did I do a good job?" Mindy asked.

Sam chuckled, a slightly forced sound. "There was usually more frosting and decoration than cookie. You were little. But Mom loved the cookies you decorated and always made me take a picture."

"I remember those pictures!" Mindy said. "Can we look at them later?"

"Of course, honey." Sam leaned closer to put an arm around Mindy and give her a side hug, and Susan's heart melted a little.

"That reminds me, I want to take some pictures today," Ralph said, "maybe out by the pool."

The conversation got more general, then, and the awkwardness passed.

Later, Susan insisted on doing the dishes so that the family could gather out by the pool.

But after a couple minutes, Helen came back in. "I didn't want you to put things away in the wrong place," she said.

"Oh…thanks." That was a backhanded offer of help if Susan had ever heard one.

"Marie always had this kitchen organized so perfectly, but every time I come it's more messed up."

Susan's hands tightened on the platter she was washing. "I'm sure it's hard for Sam to manage the house along with his business."

"It's not Sam's job to manage." The remark sounded pointed.

Susan lifted her eyebrows at the woman, wondering where this was going. "If not Sam's, then whose?"

"Well, I just hope you're not thinking it's *your* job."

"Of course not!" Susan burst out. Where did Helen get off, coming over and criticizing the help? She wasn't Susan's boss!

She glanced over at the older woman and noticed that her eyes were shiny with tears, and everything started to make sense. Helen didn't want the kitchen arrangements to change, because she was trying to preserve her daughter's memory. But inevitably, things would get moved around, and sentimental treasures mis-placed. Life had to go on, but for a grieving mother, every change must feel like losing another piece of her daughter. "Look, I'm sorry," she said, drying her hands and walking over to give the woman she barely knew a clumsy little pat on the arm. "It's a loss I can't even imagine."

"It's just hard to see another woman in her place," Helen said in a wobbly voice.

"I'm not trying to take her place," Susan said, feeling her way. "No one can do that, but especially not me. I'm just here for the summer."

"You're just not the kind of woman Sam and Mindy need."

Susan blew out a breath and plunked the platter down on the counter. Grief was one thing, but outright rudeness was another. "Did you…did you want to talk, or would you rather be alone?"

"Alone," Helen croaked out, dabbing at her eyes with a tissue.

"Sure. You go ahead and put stuff away wherever you want. I've got some reading to do." Half-guiltily, she fled the kitchen and made her way to her apartment via the front door, the better to avoid Sam and Mindy and Ralph.

Helen was right. Susan *wasn't* the kind of woman Sam and Mindy needed. But why that truth felt so hurtful, she didn't have a clue.

Chapter Five

Sam pulled into his driveway the next Friday afternoon, right after lunchtime. It would be good to get out of this monkey suit and work the rest of the rainy afternoon at home. He had a little planning to do on the summer picnic he put on for his employees, but it was all fairly low-key; Mindy could interrupt without bothering him.

And he had to admit to himself that seeing Susan was part of what had drawn him home. Not really seeing her, he told himself, but rather, seeing how she was interacting with Mindy.

He'd been so busy the past week, catching up on all the work he'd put off during the no-nanny period, that he hadn't spent a lot of time at home. Mindy seemed happy and Susan had said things were going well. He knew they'd visited the library and gone to the park with a couple of other kids. One day, Mindy had had her friend Mercedes over to play.

Sam was feeling pleased with the solution he'd come up with for Mindy's summer. She seemed to be thriving under the supervision of an active and engaged nanny.

Susan herself seemed guarded, but he had to assume she'd get more comfortable as the summer went on. That Sunday dinner with Ralph and Helen had been awkward, but that was because they hadn't understood that Susan was only a temporary fixture in the home. Next time would surely be better.

When he got inside, the sound of a busy, humming household met his ears, confirming his satisfaction with the arrangements he'd made for Mindy. He stopped in the kitchen to look at the mail, and the sound of voices drifted his way.

He heard his nephew, Xavier, explaining the finer points of Chutes and Ladders to Mindy. That meant Xavier's little sister, Baby Emmie, must be here, too, but he didn't hear baby fussing or cooing; apparently she was sleeping or content.

The low, steady murmur of women's voices

let him know that his sister-in-law and Susan were both in the room with the kids.

"I know I can talk them into it," Susan was saying doubtfully. "The payment will just be a week late, maybe ten days. It's tips versus wages, that's all. I expected to have a little more money by now."

"Troy and I could probably loan you the—"

"No! Thanks, but I'll be fine."

Angelica made some sound as if she was comforting a baby, which she probably was. "What's your mom going to do with your brother away?"

"Enjoy her freedom. And I'm hoping I can send her a plane ticket later in the summer."

"That's so nice she's coming to visit you!"

"Oh, she's not visiting me," Susan said, sounding alarmed. "I want her to be able to go to New York to see some shows, or to a nice spa. Coming to see me would be nothing but stress."

"I doubt that. You're her daughter! Or…are things bad between you?"

Sam took a step closer and leaned on the counter, eavesdropping unabashedly. Mindy and Xavier argued a little in the background. Sam could smell the remains of a mac-and-cheese lunch. He saw the tell-tale blue-and-white boxes in the trash and shook his head, a grin crossing his face. Susan hadn't claimed to be a cook.

"I'm…a bit of a disappointment to her."

"I'm sure—"

"Don't feel bad, it doesn't bother me anymore. I know she's really just upset about her own life. She had a vision for me to do a better job than she did, to be a perfect wife who made her husband happy, but I'm not falling into line."

"Well, considering that you don't have a husband at all—"

"Exactly." They both laughed.

There was a little more murmuring and the sound of a baby fussing, then some quiet shuffling.

Sam felt bad about eavesdropping, knew he should say hello to let them know he was here, but if Angelica was feeding the baby, he didn't want to intrude. Quietly, he grabbed a fork and the pan of leftover mac and cheese and picked at it, thinking about what Susan had said.

Wages versus tips. Of course, she'd been expecting to make speedy cash as a waitress. He needed to bump her paycheck forward rather than waiting the customary two weeks to pay her.

"You should just ask Sam to advance you the money," Angelica advised as if she was channeling his thoughts.

"No way! That wouldn't be right. This is a job, and you don't ask for special favors in a job."

Sam got himself a glass of water, making some noise about it, to warn everyone of his presence.

"Daddy!" Mindy called, and ran to him.

"Hey, sugar sprite. Having fun?" He swung her up into his arms, feeling that odd mixture of joy and concern that was fatherhood for him.

"Yeah! Xavier is here!"

"Go back and play with him," he said, putting her down. "I'm going to change my clothes, and then I'll want to talk to Susan a couple of minutes."

He'd move her payday up, no matter whether she protested or not. And as he trotted up the stairs, an idea came to him: he'd send her mother a go-anywhere ticket. It was a benefit of his airline program and frequent flyer miles; it wouldn't even cost him anything. And it would help out proud, independent Susan.

Which, for whatever reason, was something he very much wanted to do.

* * *

"No!" she said twenty minutes later. "I'm sorry you overheard that, but I don't need any special favors."

"It's not a favor, it's just a change in pay date." He for sure wasn't going to tell her about the ticket he'd just told his assistant to send to her mother. That would go over about as well as rat poison.

"Why are you doing this?"

"To help you out," he said patiently.

"I don't need your help!" She banged open the dishwasher and started loading dishes in. Thankfully, they were plastic ones; the china wouldn't have survived her violent treatment.

He cocked his head to one side. "I thought someone was hassling you about a late payment. If that's not the case…"

"Oh, it's true, but I can talk some sense into them. Probably."

"What's the problem? The car?" Maybe now was the time to offer her the services of his car dealer.

"No!" She scanned the now-empty counter and slammed the dishwasher shut. "My car is paid for. It's…it's my brother."

"What's wrong?"

"His camp. The last installment for this special camp I want to send him to, it's due Monday. It's why I'm working this summer. He'll just love it, and he needs the extra stimulation. And my mom needs the break." She let out an unconscious sigh, and Sam felt the strangest urge to put an arm around her.

She was a little thing to be bearing the burden for an entire family, but she didn't complain; she just accepted the responsibility. Exactly what he would have done in the same situation. Admiration rose in him, along with a strange little click of connection. Maybe he and Susan weren't as different as he'd initially thought.

"Will your first paycheck cover the payment?" he asked her.

"Just about exactly."

"Then give me the number and I'll have the money wired today."

Relief warred with resistance in her dark eyes. "But it's not fair—"

"Look," he said, "it's nothing I haven't done for other people who work for me. I take care of my employees. Go get the information."

She drew in a breath and let it out in a sigh. "All right. Thank you, Sam."

The wheels were turning in his brain now. "In fact…" he said slowly.

"What?" she asked warily.

"Do you want to earn some extra money this summer?"

She laughed, a short sound without humor. "Always. I need to send some money to my mom. And I'd love to pay for an extra course toward my master's."

"And maybe buy a new car?" he needled.

"Sam!" She put her hands on her hips. "I know my car isn't pretty, but it runs fine."

"It runs loud. And smoky."

"It's fine." She turned away. "If you're through insulting my stuff, I'd better go help Angelica with the kids."

"She's fine. Wait a minute. Listen to my proposal."

The corner of her mouth quirked upward as she spun back around. "What proposal is that?"

Their eyes met, and held, and something electric zinged between them.

The breeze through the window lifted a strand of her hair, but even as she brushed it back, she still stared at him. He could see the pulse in her neck.

His own pulse was hammering, too.

Wow.

They both looked away at the same time.

"So what are you thinking of?" she asked in a businesslike voice, grabbing a sponge to wipe down the already-clean counter.

He cleared his throat and leaned forward, resting his elbows on the kitchen island. "I'm having my annual summer picnic for my employees, and the woman who usually plans it for me is out on maternity leave. How are you at party planning?"

She laughed. "I'm a whiz with the elementary set, but I've never planned an adult party in my life."

He should definitely get someone else, then. "You could get Daisy to help," he heard himself saying. "And it's a family picnic, so we always try to make it fun for the kids. I'd pay you what I normally pay Trixi, the one on maternity leave. She gets overtime for the extra work."

"Really?" She frowned, bit her lip.

"Of course," he said, watching her, "you'd have to work pretty closely with me."

There was a beat of silence. Then: "I'm already working way too closely with you."

"What?"

She clapped her hand over her mouth. "Oh, wow, did I say that out loud?"

"Susan." He sat down on one of the bar

stools to be more at her level. She was so petite. "I hope I'm not making you uncomfortable in some way. That's the last thing I intend."

"No!" She was blushing furiously. "No, it's not that, it's just…I don't know." She turned away, staring out the window.

He came over to stand behind her, a safe couple of feet away. "I know this is pretty close quarters for two strangers. But I want you to know that I'm very pleased with your work, Susan. I think we can stop thinking of the nanny job as a trial run. I'd like for you to stay all summer."

She gripped the counter without looking at him.

"I haven't seen Mindy so happy since… well, since she was a baby and her mom was healthy."

She half looked back over her shoulder. "Really?"

The plaintive sound of her voice was so at odds with her feisty personality that he felt a strange compulsion to touch her shoulder, to run a hand over that silky hair, offering comfort.

The super-independent, super-confident teacher evidently had some vulnerabilities of her own. It almost seemed as if she hadn't received much praise, although he couldn't imagine why, when she seemed to be so good at everything she did.

Well, everything except cooking.

And why was his hand still moving toward her hair?

Just in time, he pulled it back. That wouldn't do at all.

He was getting a little too interested in Susan. She was too young, too independent, totally wrong for him in the long term, even though she was turning out to be an amazing summer nanny. He needed to get on with his program of finding Mindy a real, permanent mom. And he needed to do it soon.

He'd make sure to get back on the dating circuit right away. There were a couple of women he'd seen once and then left hanging. He'd give them a call. His secretary, who was of necessity a little too involved in his life, had a niece she wanted to fix him up with, and Mindy's Sunday school teacher had handed him her phone number along with Mindy's half-completed craft last week.

He just needed to get himself motivated to do it. He'd been too busy. But now that Susan was in place—Susan, who was completely inappropriate for him—he'd jump back into pursuing that all-important goal.

He forced himself to take a step backward. "If you're interested in the extra job, I'd appreciate having you do it. It would be easy, because you're here in the house anyway. But if you're not comfortable with it, by all means back off and I'll find someone else."

She studied him, quizzical eyes on his face, head cocked to one side. "I can give it a try," she said slowly.

And Sam tried to ignore the sudden happiness surging through him.

"When will we get to the lake, Daddy?"

Sam glanced back at Mindy, bouncing in her car seat, and smiled as he steered into the parking lot by Keystone Lake. "Hang on a minute or two, and we'll be here and out of the car."

As Mindy squealed her excitement, Sam felt tension relax out of his shoulders. Now things were falling into place.

He pulled into his old parking spot, surveying the soothing, tree-surrounded lawn with satisfaction. He'd grown up with Saturday trips to the lake, and he and Marie had brought Mindy here most summer weekends when she was small. He'd meant to continue the tradition, but it had fallen by the wayside… until now.

They'd play on the blanket, and have a nice picnic, and spend family time together. The only thing missing was the woman beside him. But Susan had agreed to work today in exchange for a weekday off next week. She'd fill the role temporarily, until he could get on his larger goal of finding a new mom for Mindy.

"It's a little cold for swimming," Susan said as she helped Mindy undo the buckles. "But there's a lot to do at the lake aside from swimming."

Sam's arms were loaded down with the picnic basket, blankets and a couple of lawn chairs, but looking around the stuff, he could see Mindy's lower lip sticking out.

"I want to swim!" his daughter said.

Susan nodded comfortably. "Okay. You can. I'm not going in that lake until the sun comes out, but I'll watch you."

Sam came around to the side of the car where Susan was bent over, gathering an armload of beach toys. "She can't go in the lake. It's too cold."

Mindy had already taken off for the water.

Susan pressed the beach toys into his already overloaded arms. "She'll figure that out for herself!" she called over her shoulder as she raced after Mindy. "Relax, Sam!"

Sam gritted his teeth, dumped the gear on a picnic table, and hustled after them.

Mindy was already up to her knees in the water. She looked back toward the shore, her expression defiant.

He opened his mouth, but Susan's hand on his arm stopped him. "It's called natural consequences," she said. "If she goes in, she'll get cold and come out quickly. No harm, no foul. And she learns something."

"But she'll catch a cold!"

Susan shrugged. "I actually think colds come from viruses, but whatever. A cold never hurt anyone."

"For a nanny, you're not very protective."

"For a successful entrepreneur, you're not much of a risk taker."

They glared at each other for a minute.

"Come in, Daddy!" Mindy called.

"No way!" He looked at his shivering daughter and took a step forward.

"Then I'll come out," Mindy decided, and splashed her way to the shoreline.

Susan gave him an I-told-you-so grin. "What are you waiting for, Dad? Get her a towel. She's freezing!"

As Sam jogged off toward the beach bags, he couldn't help smiling. A trip to the lake with Susan was never going to be dull.

After Mindy was toweled off and building a sandcastle under Susan's supervision, Sam set up the colorful beach tent they'd always used to protect Mindy's tender skin. Then he rummaged for the tablecloth, but it was no-where in sight.

Nor was the picnic. Had Susan forgotten to pack it?

Don't be controlling, he reminded him-self. Maybe she thought packing food for a Saturday beach trip was beyond her regular duties. They could always call Daisy and ask her to bring something, or as a last resort, could get something from the junk food stand at the other end of the beach.

Noticing that several children had gathered around Susan and Mindy, he strolled down to see what was going on. The little group had already created a somewhat complicated castle with the help of Mindy's multiple beach buck-ets and molds.

Mindy held a bucket with her half arm and shoved sand in with her whole one, attracting the attention of the two visiting boys.

"How come you only have one hand?" one of the boys asked Mindy.

"This is how I was born," she answered simply.

"That's weird," the child said.

Color rose on the back of Mindy's neck, and Sam opened his mouth to yell at the kid, and then closed it again. He was learning from Susan that he needed to wait and watch sometimes, rather than intervening, but when someone made a comment about his kid, it was hard. Natural consequences and learning better social skills were all well and good, but insults, not so much.

He looked at Susan to find her watching the kids with a slightly twisted mouth.

"Yeah, it's really weird," said the other boy, and they both started to laugh.

"That's enough!" Susan stepped toward them and squatted down, a protective hand on Mindy's shoulder.

"It's bullying," Mindy said. "Right, Miss Hayashi?" She'd automatically reverted to Susan's professional name, maybe because bullying was something they talked about in school.

"Very good, Mindy. You're right." Susan turned a steely glare on the two young offenders. "And bullies can't play. Goodbye, boys."

"Aw, I didn't want to play with her anyway," said one of the boys. He jumped up and ran toward the water.

"I didn't mean to be a bully," the other boy said, looking stricken. "I'm sorry."

Susan looked at Mindy. "What do you think? Can he still play, or would you rather he goes away?"

Mindy considered. "He said he was sorry."

"Yes, he did."

"He can play," Mindy decided.

"Thanks!" And the two of them were back to building a castle as if nothing had happened, while the other boy kicked stones on the beach, alone.

Susan stood and backed a little bit away, keeping her eyes on the scene as another little girl joined the group. She ended up right next to Sam.

"You did a good job handling that," he said to her, sotto voce. "I want to strangle anyone who teases my kid."

"Believe me, I felt the same way." She smiled up at him.

There was that little click of awareness between them again. She looked away first, her cheeks turning pink.

He needed to nip that attraction in the bud.

He needed to start dating, before he did something silly like let Susan know that he found her…interesting.

As he was casting about in his mind for a new subject, Mindy looked up at them. "I'm hungry," she announced.

"Well, I think we forgot a picnic," he said tactfully.

"No, I brought stuff." Susan said. "Come on over, we'll have lunch."

"I'm hungry, too," said the little girl who'd just joined in the group.

"Me, too!" The little boy stood up and brushed sand off his hands onto his swim trunks.

"Tell you what, go ask your mom or dad if you can share our lunch," Susan said easily.

"Do we have enough?" Sam hadn't seen evidence of *any* food, so the thought of sharing was puzzling.

"Oh, sure," she said as the children ran toward their separate families. "It'll be fine."

He didn't see how, but he followed Susan and Mindy, curious to see what she came up with.

From the bottom of the bag of beach toys, she tugged a loaf of whole wheat bread, a tub of peanut butter, and a squeeze bottle of grape jelly. "Voila," she said as the other two kids approached. "Let's play 'make your own sandwich!'"

"Yay!" cheered the kids.

Sam frowned at the splintery picnic table, thinking of the neat checkered tablecloth Marie had always brought to the lake. "It's not very clean."

She was digging again in the toy bag and didn't hear him. "Hey, Sam, grab me one of those beach towels, could you? Oh, there we go." Triumphantly, she produced a small stack of paper cups.

He handed a towel to her and she spread it over the table. "Everybody, take a cup. We'll wash hands and then get water from the drinking fountain." She looked at Sam. "Coming?"

"So lunch is…peanut butter sandwiches and water?"

She seemed genuinely puzzled. "You were expecting caviar?"

"No, but maybe…never mind." He didn't elaborate on checkered tablecloths and homemade chicken salad and cut up melon in a special blue bowl, but for a second, his whole chest hurt with missing his wife.

Mindy was tugging at his hand. "Come on, Daddy, I'm hungry!"

The next fifteen minutes were a blur of helping a bunch of primary-school-aged kids make messy PB&J sandwiches and chatting with the parents who came over to check everything out. Both families, it turned out, knew Susan from the school, and showed respect for her and interest in her summer plans.

Finally the kids headed back to the water with one of the other families, and he and Susan collapsed down onto the picnic bench. Susan cut the sandwich she'd managed to make for herself and offered him half.

To his surprise, it actually tasted good.

"What I wouldn't give for a cup of coffee," she admitted.

"I could buy you one at the refreshment stand, since you provided the lunch," he offered.

"Well, technically you provided it. But if you'll buy me a coffee I'll follow you anywhere."

"Anywhere?" he asked lightly as they stood up together.

"Maybe." She had the cutest way of wrinkling her nose.

And he needed to watch it, or he'd be getting those romantic feelings for her again. He pulled himself together, checked one last time on Mindy, and then led the way to the concession area.

They were halfway across the grassy lawn when a young guy tossed a ball straight at Susan.

Sam stepped forward, ready to slug the guy, but Susan had already caught the ball and tossed it back, laughing. "Hey, Hunter," she said. "What's going on? Enjoying the summer off?"

The twentysomething guy rose to his feet, shirtless and in surf-style jammer shorts, and pushed his sunglasses to the top of his head. "I'd be better if you'd join the teachers' volleyball league," he said. "Every Wednesday. It's fun."

"Oh, well, I don't think so, but thanks."

"What are you doing for fun this summer?" the guy asked. Focused on Susan, he was completely ignoring Sam.

Sam restrained the urge to move closer and put a protective arm around Susan. No way could she be interested in this guy, right? He was much too young and silly.

He's Susan's age, his inner critic reminded him.

"I'm at the lake! That's fun, right?" She gestured toward a couple of people who'd headed down toward the water. "Your friends are leaving you. You'd better catch up."

"Hey, good to see you. I'll give you a call." He jogged off.

Susan rolled her eyes. "And I'll block your number," she muttered.

Relief washed over him. "You don't like him?"

She shook her head. "He's fine, but he just won't take no for an answer."

Curious now, Sam fell into step beside her. "That must be a problem, guys hitting on you."

She laughed. "No, not usually, but Hunter is fairly new in town. He doesn't know my reputation."

"What's your reputation?"

"I'm known as a cold fish." She kicked at a rock with a small, neat bare foot, toenails painted pale blue. "Or, sometimes, too mouthy and assertive. I don't get asked out a lot."

"That surprises me," Sam said, tearing his eyes away from those delicate feet. "Does it bother you?"

She shook her head. "Not really," she said. "I'm not looking for love. I'm one of those people who's meant to be single, I think."

Sam knew with everything in him that this warm, funny, kid-loving woman was meant to be a mother. And a wife. "That surprises me, too."

"Why?" she asked.

"Well, because you're…cute. And a lot of fun."

"Thanks," she said drily. "I didn't know you cared."

He lifted his hands. "I didn't mean I cared like *that*…" He felt heat rising up his neck.

She studied him sideways. "It's okay, Sam. I really have no expectations in that area. I'm not angling for a date with Rescue River's richest bachelor."

She seemed to be telling the truth, and to his surprise, he found that refreshing. A lot of the women he dated did have expectations. They liked him for his big house and his money and his CEO position. Not so much for who he was inside.

"So tell me about *your* love life," she said, seeming to read his mind. "Since I don't have one."

"Not much to tell on my side, either," he said.

She made a small sound of disagreement in her throat. "Daisy says you date women just like your wife."

He felt his face redden. "Daisy has a few too many opinions."

She chuckled. "I know what you mean. And there's nothing wrong with having a type. What was Marie like?"

He smiled, remembering, for once, with enjoyment rather than pain. "Beautiful, though she always worried about her weight. Loved being a mother more than anything else."

"I'm sure Mindy was a joy to her."

"That she was." He thought some more. "Marie was…a perfectionist. Wanted her home and her flowers and her family to be just picture-perfect."

She nodded. "How did she deal with Mindy's disability, then?"

He frowned, thinking. "She didn't want to highlight it, but she loved Mindy just as she was."

"That's good," Susan said. "Sounds like the two of you were…in sync. Perfect, loving parents."

"We were." They'd reached the food stand, and he ordered them both coffees. "We were in sync, that is. Perfect, of course not. Nobody is."

"Some people try harder at it," she said as

she stirred an inordinate amount of sugar into her coffee.

She was making him think: about his history, his relationship with Marie, his views on how life should be lived. In the past year of dating, no other woman had really got him to examine his life.

He wasn't sure if he loved it or hated it. Yet another thing to think about, but not today. "What about you?" he asked. "You seem driven in the career area of your life. Wouldn't you say you try to be perfect there?"

She shook her head. "I'm in elementary and special ed. Aiming for perfection doesn't work for us."

He eyed her narrowly. "Excellence?"

"As a teacher, I try. In my personal life...I pretty much ruled that out a long time ago."

"That's cryptic." He paused, giving her space to respond, but for whatever reason, she didn't.

They strolled together back toward the picnic table. "Mindy's having fun," Sam said, pointing to her as she splashed in the lake with her new friends. "Thanks for making this happen."

"I didn't. It was your idea."

"I know, but…for whatever reason, I don't tend to do stuff like this alone with Mindy."

"Why don't you?"

"It just doesn't seem…right. Not without Marie."

"It doesn't seem perfect?"

"I guess not."

They strolled together more slowly. "Somehow," she said, "I don't think it was just Marie who was the perfectionist. But I'll do my best to keep things together for you guys this summer, until the right woman comes along."

Chapter Six

Back at the house, after a quick dinner of beef-aroni stirred up by Sam, they watched an hour of TV. All sprawled together on the sectional sofa, Sam on one side of Mindy and Susan on the other.

Like a family. Too much so. Susan was hyperaware of Sam's warm arm, curved around Mindy but brushing against her. Of the smell of his skin, some brisk manly bodywash or deodorant he used. Of the carefree way he threw back his head and laughed at the cartoon antics on the TV screen. She liked seeing this carefree, boyish side of him. He didn't relax enough.

And wherever that wifely thought had come from, it needed to go right back there.

As the show ended, Mindy slumped to her side, asleep.

"Poor kiddo, she's exhausted," Susan said, stroking Mindy's soft hair.

Sam slid his arms underneath her. "I'll carry her upstairs. C'mon, Mindy. Time for bed."

"Miss…Susan…come," Mindy ordered sleepily.

"Do you mind?" Sam asked.

Did she mind playing the mother role, hanging out with this sweet father and daughter and falling for them more each day? "No problem," she said, and followed Sam up the stairs.

While Sam helped Mindy get ready, Susan looked around the big bedroom, really paying attention to its décor for the first time. With a Noah's Ark theme, it had a hand-painted border, and the bed was shaped like an ark. Ruffly curtains portrayed cheery pairs of animals, and a mobile dangled above the bed. It was a gorgeous room…for a three-year-old.

It made sense that Sam hadn't redecorated; that had to be the last thing on his mind, and the room was fine. But noticing all the things in this house that had frozen, at the point where a loving mother had gotten too ill to update them, made sadness push at Susan's chest.

Once Mindy was in her pajamas with teeth brushed, she was awake enough to want to talk. "That boy today was a bully," she said seriously. "Wasn't he, Miss Susan?"

Susan nodded. "He was. Did he hurt your feelings?"

"Yes. I don't like the way my arm is." Mindy held it up to look at it critically. "I wish I had two hands like other kids."

Susan glanced up in time to see pain flash across Sam's face. It must be hard to see your child suffering. And it didn't look as if Sam knew what to say.

But suddenly, Susan remembered how her own mother had talked to her about looking different. "You know," she said, "when I was a little girl, I wished I had round eyes instead of Japanese ones," she said.

"Your eyes aren't round," Mindy agreed, "but they're pretty."

"Thank you! But I still wished I looked like my mom. Even my brother came out looking more white, with round eyes. But I got my dad's Japanese look. For a while, I really hated it."

Mindy nodded, trying to understand. "What did you do?"

Susan laughed. "I did eye exercises every night, hoping I could make my eyes round. But of course, I couldn't."

"Sometimes I pull on my arm," Mindy confided, "so maybe it will grow longer."

"Mindy!" Sam sounded horrified. "That won't work, and it could hurt you."

Mindy's lip pouted out. "It *could* work."

"My eye exercises never did," Susan said. "But my mom bought me a poster for my room. It said, 'Be Your Own Kind of Beautiful.' There were pink butterflies on it." She smiled, remembering how happy the special attention from her mom had made her.

"I like butterflies. Can I have a poster like that?"

Susan raised her eyebrows at Sam, pretty sure that he'd order one before midnight struck.

"Of course you can, sweetie," he said.

"What really helped the most," Susan said, "was knowing God made me the way He did for a reason. My mom kept telling me I was part of His plan."

"God made everyone," Mindy agreed doubtfully.

"That's right." Susan patted Mindy's arm. "Also, getting some more friends who looked like me helped a lot, too. I could see I wasn't alone, or strange."

"Nobody else has a short arm," Mindy said.

"Oh, yes, they do. In fact, when we go to

the library next week, we'll see if Miss Fern can order us some books about kids with limb differences."

Mindy's eyes were closing. "'Kay," she said. "Can you sing for me, Miss Susan?"

Sing? Susan couldn't restrain a chuckle. "Oh, honey, you don't want me to sing. Maybe Daddy could sing for you."

"Mommy and Daddy...used to sing...together."

Susan drew in a breath and let it out in a sigh and looked at Sam. So much grief in this house. So much healing to do. So many ways she'd never live up to the perfect Marie, not even as a summer nanny. "Go for it, Dad," she said.

Sam cleared his throat, his face closed. "We'll sing tomorrow, sweetheart."

Susan thought to flick on the little music player beside the bed, and some lullabies, meant for a younger child, poured out.

A quiet moment later, Mindy was asleep.

With a glance at each other, Sam and Susan rose at the same moment and tiptoed from the room. As they walked quietly down the stairs, she glanced up at him. "Sorry I can't sing."

"You bring other strengths," he said. "That

really helped, what you said to her about wanting to be different from how you are."

"She should definitely meet other kids with limb differences." Susan felt relieved as they eased into a more businesslike topic. "I'll do a little research tomorrow, see what's out there. Angelica said something about a camp for kids with special needs."

"Great. But hey," he said, putting a hand on her shoulder, "did you really want your eyes to be different, or was that just for Mindy's benefit?"

"I wanted it. Every little girl wants to look like her mommy."

His grip tightened on her shoulder, and he turned her toward him. One hand cupped the side of her face, and his thumb touched the corner of her eye with a gentle caress. "I, for one, think your eyes are beautiful just as they are."

Susan went still, but inside, her heart was pounding out of control. She stared up at him, unable to speak.

He smiled, his own eyes crinkling. "Thanks for today."

"It was good to be with you and Mindy."

They were frozen there, in a moment that seemed to last forever, looking at each other. Lullabies sounded quietly from upstairs, and

Susan breathed in the soap-and-aftershave scent that was Sam. She tipped her head a little to feel more of the hand that still rested on her cheek.

And then the front door opened, letting in the most unwelcome sound in the world. "Hey, yoo-hoo!"

It was Helen. Susan stepped back guiltily. Sam let his hand drop.

And they came down the steps double time, but not before Mindy's grandmother had appeared at the landing and seen them, her husband close behind her.

And not before Susan caught sight of the giant portrait of Sam, Mindy and the perfect Marie, directly at the bottom of the stairs.

"Just let me know what it costs," Sam said, and Susan looked at him, puzzled.

"That camp for special-needs kids," he explained.

"Oh!" Susan nodded. "You're fine with her going?"

"Sure, fine," he said, trotting the rest of the way down the stairs, obviously having no idea of what he'd just agreed to.

"Mindy isn't special needs." Helen eyed them suspiciously. "What's been going on?"

Way too much, Susan wanted to say as she

followed Sam. Too much emotion for a little family that wasn't hers and never would be. A family that had a perfect woman always in the background.

She was starting to see that she might be able to fit into a family, that she might have something to offer, despite her lack of domestic skills. Part of that was Sam's appreciation for what she offered to a child like Mindy.

But she wasn't what he wanted. He wanted another Marie.

And he wasn't what she wanted, either, she reminded herself. She didn't want a businessman like her dad and her ex-fiancé, who would have overly high expectations and just throw money at any problem that arose.

"Sam," Helen said, "We stopped over to invite you to the Fourth of July picnic next week at the country club. There's someone I want you to meet." Her voice was rich with innuendo, and she was practically waggling her eyebrows at Sam.

"Mindy and I always go," Sam said, looking uncomfortable. "Surely you didn't come here just to invite me to that?"

"Oh, my, no. Come on, sit down." Helen led the way to the kitchen and pulled a sheaf of papers out of her large purse. Susan, feeling unwelcome but unsure of what to do, followed along behind them.

"There's all this paperwork for the Little Miss Rescue River Pageant. It's got to be filled out this week. I thought I could help you get Mindy signed up." She held up a brochure portraying a little girl dressed in a super-fancy evening dress.

"A beauty pageant?" Susan couldn't keep the derisive squeak out of her voice.

But Helen didn't seem to notice. "Yes, it's so much fun. I'm on the planning committee, and we've been busy setting up a wonderful show." Her voice was animated, her eyes lively.

"Oh, it's a big to-do," Ralph contributed.

Susan looked at Sam. Was he on board with this?

Thankfully, he was shaking his head. "It's a great event, but I'm not sure Mindy's ready…" He trailed off and sat down at the counter.

"But she's about to turn six, which is the lower age limit. I'm so happy that she can finally join in the fun!" Helen's voice was determinedly peppy, as if she was getting ready to run right over Sam.

And Sam, the big tough businessman, looked about to cave.

Susan jumped in. "I don't think that would be good for Mindy."

All eyes turned her way.

"Why on earth not?" Helen glared at her.

Could the woman really have no clue? "Beauty pageants force little girls to dress in age-inappropriate clothes and focus only on their appearance. There's research that shows they foster eating disorders and an unhealthy dependence on external validation."

"You could use a little more focus on *your* appearance," Helen said, eyeing Susan's cut-offs and T-shirt with disdain.

Ouch! Susan clamped her mouth shut to avoid saying something she couldn't take back, and surprising, unwelcome tears pushed at her eyes. Her self-image had improved since the days when she'd hated the way she looked, but it still wasn't perfect.

"Hey, hey now." Sam held up a hand. "Susan, Mindy and I dressed for a day at the lake, and we look it. Nothing wrong with that."

Helen muttered something that might have been "Sorry."

Susan made a little sound in her throat that might pass for "okay." But it wasn't. She didn't like Helen one bit.

"Let's keep the focus on Mindy," Sam went on. "I just worry, Helen, that with her hand—"

"She could carry something to cover it if she wanted, or wear gloves," Helen said. "You know what a mix the pageant is. Everything from casual and relaxed to hairpieces and fake teeth."

"Exactly! It's a huge fake thing." Susan thought of the little girl sleeping upstairs, pulling on her hand to try to make it look like other children's. "It's an outdated ritual, and it would be bad for Mindy. Have you ever watched *Tiny Tot Beauty*?"

"Susan, it's not that kind of thing." Sam looked distinctly uncomfortable.

She understood. It was hard for him to stand up to Mindy's overbearing grandmother. But she herself had no such qualms. "Have you seen what pageant people are like? What can those parents be thinking, pushing their little kids into that high-glamour lifestyle? I mean, I'm sure this small-town pageant isn't as bad as the big pageants you see on reality TV, but it's a step in the wrong direction."

The room was silent around her.

"Right?" she said, looking at Sam.

"Susan," he said quietly, "Marie was in pageants."

"Yep," Ralph said, nodding. "Those big ones.

There wasn't reality TV back in those days, but I've watched the shows. They pretty much tell it like it was for us."

"Oh." Oops. Susan blew out her breath, her face heating.

Helen didn't say anything. Not in words, anyway, but her glare said it all.

Without meaning to, Susan had shot daggers at the woman they all loved so much. The woman Sam had adored and still did. The mother little Mindy aspired to look like and never would. Never would even see again.

They were all looking at her.

When would she ever learn to shut her mouth? "I'm sorry. I'm sure I…don't know everything about pageants. In fact, I probably know a lot less than anyone else in this room, so…" She trailed off into the silence.

The doorbell provided a welcome distraction. "Let me get that," she said.

"She certainly makes herself at home in your house," Susan heard Helen say as she left the room.

"Got some opinions, too," Ralph said.

As she hurried to the door, Susan's face felt as if it was on fire.

She opened it to a welcome sight: Daisy.

"Hey girl, I knocked on your apartment door

and when I didn't find you, I figured you must be over here." She squinted at Susan. "Looks like you could use some girl talk."

"More than you know. Let me grab my stuff." She hurried into the kitchen for her beach bag, cell phone and keys as Daisy chatted with Helen.

Five minutes later they were drinking sodas in Susan's tiny living room. "How's it going?" Daisy asked. "You surviving the dragon lady?"

"She didn't like me before," Susan said, "but after tonight, she hates me." She told Daisy about the beauty pageant fiasco. "So if there was any hope of our getting along, not that it really matters, it went out the window tonight."

"She thinks you're after Sam," Daisy said, nodding shrewdly.

"What? Why would she think that?" Even as she spoke, Susan felt her face flush, remembering that moment on the stairs.

If Helen hadn't come, would he have kissed her?

Would she have let him?

Daisy eyed her suspiciously. "What's going on?"

Susan shook her head. Daisy was her best friend, but no way was she going to share the occasional moments of strange attraction between her and Daisy's big brother.

Instead, she turned the topic back to the pageant Helen wanted Mindy to enter.

Daisy rolled her eyes. "I'm with you. Pageants are pretty ridiculous most of the time. But the Rescue River one isn't so bad."

Susan couldn't restrain her curiosity. "Was Marie really a pageant kid? Like on *Tiny Tot Beauty?*"

"Yep. She was way into it, through middle school at least. I'm sure there are some pictures around." Daisy cocked her head to one side, thinking. "In fact, Helen might have been in some pageants, too, back in the day."

Susan groaned. "So it's a family tradition, and I interfered with it with all my big California ideas. Sam's probably getting ready to fire me right now."

Daisy laughed. "Sam can take it. In fact, I think you're good for him. He looks more relaxed than usual. Even seems to have a bit of a tan."

"We were at the lake today," Susan explained, and told her about their day.

Daisy crossed her arms and studied Susan, her expression curious. "Sounds pretty cozy. How do you feel about Sam, anyway?"

"He's a good employer, and we're getting along better than I expected."

"Are you sure that's all there is to it? I mean, Sam's incredibly handsome, and has a great big heart, and he's also the richest man in town. Any chance of you falling for him?"

"No!" Susan held up a hand to stop Daisy's protest. "I don't date, remember? I'm committed to staying single so I can focus on my career. Plus," she added, "if I were going to go out with someone, it wouldn't be one of those classic business types. I like quirky, creative guys, and Sam's anything but."

"Does your dad's treatment of your family have to affect you forever?" Daisy asked bluntly.

"My dad's…what do you mean?" She didn't like the way Daisy was looking at her, as if she was a social work client. A troubled one.

"Our childhoods have an impact," Daisy lectured, in full counselor mode. "You think Sam is too much like your dad, but he's not only a businessman. He's a brother and a dad. And he's very lonely."

"He misses his wife, I can tell that." Susan frowned. "Even if I *were* interested—and I'm not—it would be crazy to get involved with a family still grieving such a big loss. They'd rip my heart out."

Daisy looked thoughtful. "I know Sam seems obsessed with Marie, but appearances can be deceptive. He's trying to keep her memory alive for Mindy, and he's been too busy surviving to build them a new life. But I can see him changing, letting go."

Susan walked over to the kitchen and snagged the jumbo bag of spicy tortilla chips. "Don't you think they need some counseling?" she asked as she replenished the bowl on the coffee table.

"They've had it. Do you think I would've let them muddle through without help? But it's a process." Daisy grabbed a chip and munched it, thoughtfully, then spoke again. "And you have to remember that Jesus can heal. He can heal Sam and Mindy of what they lost when Marie died. And He can heal you from the way your father treated you."

Susan leaned her head back on the couch and stared up at the ceiling fan. She wanted to believe it. She wished for Daisy's faith. But it was a stretch right now. "I'm afraid to change," she admitted. "I've been committed to being a single schoolteacher for so long. I've felt like that's God's will for me."

"His will might be bigger than you can imagine right now. Maybe it involves getting married, having kids of your own *and* being a schoolteacher. Ever think of that?"

Susan *had* thought of it lately. Specifically in connection to Sam and Mindy. But the whole idea felt risky and dangerous and scary. "It's out of my comfort zone. What with my family and all."

"God kinda specializes in out-of-our-comfort-zone."

Susan thought about that. God had called her to work with special-needs kids—in the classroom, or so she'd thought. But she knew she was doing good for Mindy right now. Taking this job with Sam had been a risk, but she could see that it was paying off. At least for Mindy, which was the important thing.

"And," Daisy continued, frowning, "it might be time for Sam to take down a few pictures from the Marie gallery. I'll talk to him about it." She grabbed Susan's hand. "But you need to work on healing, too. You're not limited to your past. With God's help, you can have a bright future and you can have love."

"But I don't want—"

"Just think about it."

Night was falling, turning the summer sky to pinks and purples, sending a cool breeze fragrant with honeysuckle through the open window.

Susan heard a car door slam outside. Hopefully, that was Helen and Ralph, leaving.

"Promise me you'll think and pray about healing, okay? Not just so you can work something out with Sam, although that would be totally cool. But no matter what happens with him, I want to see you be happy and whole."

Susan hugged her friend. "Thanks for caring about me. I know Jesus can heal. I know it in my head. But I'm not quite there with believing it in my heart."

After that emotional night, Susan and Sam steered a little clear of each other, seemingly by mutual agreement. When Susan had a question about the company picnic she was planning, she mostly texted Sam and he responded with brief, impersonal instructions.

She did notice that Sam quietly took down some of the Marie pictures, replacing them with drawings Mindy had made, which he'd had beautifully framed, and more recent photographs of him and Mindy. The change, Susan was sure, was Daisy's doing; she must have had that talk with Sam.

He'd also spent a couple of evenings helping Mindy create a photo album of her mother and her, which Mindy had proudly showed Susan each morning after Sam went to work.

Susan was surprised and impressed. Sam definitely had a stubborn, bossy side, but he also was able to listen to his sister's wisdom and follow it, and his thoughtfulness with his daughter, his intelligent care of her, made him all the more appealing.

She found herself watching him sometimes, in a silly, romantic way that wasn't doing her heart any good at all.

She just needed to keep reminding herself that her goal wasn't to swoon over her boss's softer side. It was to fix her own family's problems while staying independent. She wasn't the marrying kind, and in a tempting situation like this, she had to keep that well in mind.

Sam had brushed aside her apologies about her awkward words to his in-laws, saying everything was fine. But it wasn't, Susan could tell. He'd been distant, and she felt bad about it. Who was she to judge how others lived their lives? Maybe there was some redeeming value in pageants she didn't understand. And in any case, it wasn't her business. She was just the nanny.

She and Mindy were finger-painting late one afternoon when her phone buzzed. She washed her hands and looked at the text message. From Sam, and her heart jumped.

Did you get my message before?

Susan looked and started to sweat.

Hate to ask but could you fix something easy for dinner? Job candidate here with wife and two active boys. Would like to invite them home. Nothing special, no stress. ETA 5 p.m.

No stress. Ha! She checked the message again. Yes, it did say they'd arrive at 5.

It was 4:15.

She drew in a breath and sat up straighter. Here was her chance to impress Sam with her domestic abilities and make up for being such a screw-up the other night.

No problem, she texted back. She'd disappointed him then, but she wouldn't do it again. She could get it done.

"Come on, Mindy," she said. "We have work to do."

When Sam arrived home promptly at 4:55, he had a little trepidation as he held the car door for Emily, his job candidate's wife.

"Wow, that's a big house!" cried one of the couple's twin boys. They were cute, freckle-faced redheads with energy to burn, probably a couple years older than Mindy.

"How many kids do you have?" the other twin asked.

"One, and she should be inside. Come on in."

Just then, Susan came around the side of the house. She wore neat shorts and a…was that a golf shirt? He'd never have guessed she owned anything so plain and ordinary.

She didn't look like herself, quite; she looked…almost traditional. A thought crossed his mind: had she dressed that way for him?

Surely she wouldn't do that, but the very notion of it tugged at his heart. If she'd tried to look conservative for him, it was a totally endearing effort.

And she should probably remove some of her multiple earrings to complete the effect.

"Come around back," she said. "Every-thing's ready."

"I can get the drinks," Sam said, relief washing over him at her gracious greeting. Times like this, he really needed a wife, and Susan was acting like a good stand-in. He wanted to bring Bill in as CEO of his agricultural real estate division, which would free Sam up to focus on the land management side of the business—and to spend a little less time at the office. But Bill and Emily were city people, used to sophisticated living, so he was going to have to sell them hard on the virtues of Rescue River.

On the back deck, overlooking the pool, the table was set with a red checkered tablecloth and there were baskets of potato chips and dip. Retro, casual, but that was okay. He'd only let Susan know today.

Burgers were on the grill, smelling great, and through the open kitchen window, peppy jazz played. Nice.

Mindy came out, carefully carrying a bowl of baby carrots. A glass bowl, but Sam restrained himself from helping her. She was adept with her hand and half arm, and he was learning, from Susan, to let her do as much as possible on her own. He introduced her to the boys and the adults and she greeted everyone politely and turned away. "'Scuse me, I gotta bring the dip."

Susan emerged with a bin of assorted soft drinks on ice, and since everyone seemed to enjoy choosing their own, he didn't even complain about the fact that they were drinking from cans. It was a barbecue, he told himself. Relax.

Susan looked extremely cute. She'd tied a barbecue apron over her shorts and shirt and was concentrating on the burgers. "Hey, I think these are done already," she said, and they all sat down.

Dinner was happening a little too quickly, and he wanted to suggest that everyone needed to enjoy their sodas and relax a bit before eating.

"Yay, I'm starving!" cried one of the boys.

"Me, too!" yelled his brother.

Their mother smiled, so Sam let it go.

It was make-your-own-burgers—again, a little too casual for his tastes, but the family seemed fine with it. Susan ducked back into the kitchen and emerged with a casserole dish which, when she opened it, contained macaroni and cheese that looked suspiciously like the kind from a box. He arched an eyebrow at her.

"Mac and cheese!" the boys shouted.

"I really appreciate your arranging this to be so kid-friendly," the job candidate, Bill, said to Susan.

She chuckled, a throaty sound that tickled Sam's nerve endings. "Casual and kid-friendly, that's my specialty," she said with an apologetic smile to Sam.

Sam offered up a quick prayer and then they all dug in.

Sam took a giant bite of hamburger. His teeth hit something hard and he tasted ice.

Quickly he put the burger down. "I don't think these are done. Better get them back on the grill," he said.

Susan's face flamed. "Oh, no, I'm sorry. They came right out of the freezer, but I thought, with the grill so hot…"

Bill grinned. "Mistake of a novice griller," he said.

"I don't like hamburgers," announced one of the boys. "I like hot dogs better."

"Me, too!" Mindy said.

"We do have some," Susan said hesitantly. "I'm sorry, Sam."

Sam slapped a mosquito and noticed Mindy and the quieter little boy were doing the same. "Couldn't you find the bug torches?" he asked Susan.

"I…never heard of bug torches," she said regretfully. "Look. I'll grab the hot dogs, and we'll put the burgers back on the grill. You guys go hunt down the bug torches because I, for one, am getting eaten alive."

Everyone got up from the table and went to their respective stations. Sam was shaking his head. If there had ever been a worse attempt at impressing a prospective employee, he didn't know what it was.

"Sorry," she whispered as she brushed past him. And even amidst his annoyance, he felt a rush of sympathy and patted her shoulder.

"Can I come in and help?" asked Emily, a very quiet woman.

Susan shrugged resignedly. "If you want. It's a huge mess inside."

"We'll come, too!" the ginger-haired twins said and rushed inside.

As they walked to the garage, Bill clapped him on the back. "Ask me sometime to tell you about my major disaster of a client dinner," he said.

When they got the torches lit, everyone was still in the house, and the sound of the boys' yelling rang through the open windows. With some trepidation, Sam pushed in, followed by his client. And stopped and stared.

The entire kitchen table was covered with paint pots and paper, and the two visiting boys were having a heyday with it. The mother, who seemed to lack discipline or authority, was scolding ineffectually, and the boys were ignoring her.

"Those are *my* finger paints," Mindy said, looking ready to blow.

Susan was arm-deep in the refrigerator. "I know there are some hot dogs in here somewhere," she was saying.

What a disaster!

The doorbell rang. "Mindy, could you or your daddy get that?" Susan called, obviously glad to have found Mindy a distraction.

Sam started to follow Mindy, but when he saw who'd arrived, he went back to the kitchen to give himself time to take a deep breath.

He needed it.

His daughter came in a moment later with Sam's father, who'd started Hinton Enterprises as a small agricultural real estate firm fifty years ago. "It's Grandpa!" she announced.

Sam felt a rush of the inadequacy he'd grown up with. His father was hard to please and, since he'd met Bill earlier in the day, he knew this dinner should be impressive. Sam was making a mess of things.

"Boys!" Bill scolded, frowning at his own wife.

"What on earth is going on?" Mr. Hinton asked.

Sam blew out a breath, looked around and realized he was going to have to take charge.

But there was a touch on his arm, one that tingled. Susan. "Sorry," she mouthed to him.

And then she proceeded to take charge herself. "Boys!" she said in a firm, quiet voice accompanied by a hand-clap. "Finger paints are for after dinner. Mindy, please show your new friends how to wash their hands at the kitchen sink."

"Marie never would have allowed that," Mr. Hinton said in a voice that was meant to be quiet but wasn't.

Sam saw a muscle twitch in Susan's face. She was no dummy. She knew she was being compared.

She drew in a breath. "Mr. Hinton, here." She put two packages of hot dogs into his hands. "You're in charge of grilling these. Sam." She handed him two packages of buns. "Take these outside, along with your clients. Socialize. Do your thing."

She turned to the children, who stood quietly watching her, obviously recognizing that teacher voice. In fact, Sam thought, even his father seemed to recognize that voice. "Kids, you can play outside with Mindy's toys until dinner. After you eat your hot dogs..." She tapped a finger on her lips. "I think we've got some of Xavier's clothes here. You can put on swimsuits or shorts, and finger-paint for a bit, and then jump in the pool to clean up. If that's okay with Mom?" She looked questioningly at Emily.

"Of course. Thank you."

"Yay!" cried the boys, and all three kids rushed outside.

So the men bonded over how to re-cook half-frozen, half-burnt burgers with ketchup already on them, and they grilled up a bunch of hot dogs. The kids played while Susan talked with Emily, who gradually became more animated. Dinner was eaten half at the table and half by the pool, and Sam's father actually stayed to eat three of the hot dogs he'd cooked and then to sit on a chaise lounge by the pool, watching the kids play.

The sun peeked through the clouds on its way toward the horizon, turning the sky rosy and sending beams of golden light that, as a kid, he'd always thought seemed to come directly from God. Salted caramel ice cream topped with chocolate syrup from a squirt bottle made a fine dessert, to his surprise. As the evening grew chilly, Susan brought out a heap of old sweatshirts from the front closet, and everyone put them on and stayed outside, talking and laughing.

Gradually, Sam relaxed. It wasn't exactly orthodox, but the prospective employee's family seemed to be having a good time.

When darkness fell and the kids climbed out of the pool, shivering, Susan wrapped them in towels and took all of them inside to dress, accompanied by the mother.

"I tell you what," Bill said as he and Sam stood on the front porch. "When I saw this big house, I thought, oh, man, too rich for our blood. We like to keep it simple. But this has been great." He pumped Sam's hand as his wife and tired children came out onto the porch. "I've made my decision. I like this town and this lifestyle. If you still want me after the way my kids have behaved, I'd like to come work for Hinton Enterprises."

Fifteen minutes later, Sam stood with his father, watching the family drive away. "That's the wackiest business dinner I ever witnessed," Mr. Hinton said, clapping Sam on the shoulder. "But whatever works, son." He gave Sam a squinty-eyed glare. "You're not thinking about marrying that Japanese girl, are you?"

"Her name's Susan," Sam said. "And no. Nothing like that. I have other plans for that side of my life."

His father nodded. "Best to get moving on

them. That little girl of yours isn't getting any younger. Seems to me she needs some brothers and sisters to play with."

"Yes, sir, I'm aware of that." He knew the clock was ticking. And every minute he spent noticing the appeal of an unconventional schoolteacher with a knack for causing disasters, even if they did usually turn out just fine, was a minute he wasn't finding the proper sort of mother for his daughter.

Was a minute he spent *not* fulfilling his promise to Marie.

The next Friday, July Fourth, Susan helped Mindy dress in her new red, white and blue shorts and shirt to go to the country club picnic. The day had dawned bright and hot, perfect weather for a picnic.

She was *not* looking forward to this.

She didn't need to spend the time with Sam, who'd been surprisingly kind about her disastrous efforts to cook dinner for his job candidate's family. He hadn't had a lot to say over the past few days, but she sensed that his attitude toward her had softened.

Which made him even more appealing. But she had to guard her heart. She didn't need to fall for a guy who wanted something altogether different in a woman. She wasn't going to put herself through that again.

"I'm bored," Mindy announced.

There was still an hour until it was time to leave, so Susan took her charge downstairs and looked around for something to occupy her. They'd spent enough time in the playroom, and the formal living room had too many breakables to be a good play area.

"Let's check our seedlings," she suggested, and they went to the kitchen window. To Mindy's delight, tiny, bent plants were appearing in the soil they'd put in an egg carton.

"They're not very green," Mindy said, poking at one with her finger.

"They need more light. Let's find another window to put them in."

They each took an egg carton and wandered around the mansion's downstairs, looking for the perfect spot. It occurred to Susan that she'd never been inside the sunroom. Even though she'd seen it from outside, the blinds had always been drawn. "Come on, Mindy," she said. "Let's try in here."

Mindy emerged from the formal dining room, saw Susan's hand on the doorknob of the sunroom. "No!" she shrieked, dropping her egg carton. "Don't go in there!"

Susan spun back toward the little girl, less concerned with the dirt and seedlings now soiling the cream-colored carpet than about Mindy's frantic expression. "Hey," she said, putting down her egg carton and kneeling in front of Mindy. "What's wrong?"

"Don't go in there, don't go in there," the child said anxiously, her eyes round.

"Okay, I won't," Susan promised. "But why?"

Mindy's face reddened and her eyes filled with tears. "I don't like that room."

"Okay, okay. Shh." She pulled Mindy into her arms and hugged her until some of the tension left her body. "Come on, we'd better save our plants."

Mindy looked down, only now realizing that she'd dropped her egg-carton planter. "Oh, no, they're gonna be broken."

"I think we can save them," Susan said. "And I have a good idea about how. Come on, you can help."

Forty-five minutes later, the little plants were replanted in some old cartoon character mugs Susan had discovered in the back of a cupboard. The mess was cleaned up, though Susan was going to have to tell the cleaning service to give that area of the rug a little extra attention. And Mindy was calm again, paging quietly through a library book about plants.

As for Susan, she had to get ready. In a weak moment, she'd agreed to go to the club herself, at Daisy and Sam's insistence, so she put on her own faded "Proud to be an American" T-shirt to pair with her standard denim capris and sandals. She pulled her hair up into a ponytail and added a little mascara and blush, and at Mindy's insistence, tied a red, white and blue ribbon into her hair.

But as Sam backed the car out of the driveway, Susan couldn't help looking toward the sunroom that was visible from the side of the house.

Why was the door always closed? Why was Mindy afraid of the sunroom?

When they reached the country club, Mindy tugged Susan along, chattering a mile a minute, while Sam gathered blankets and lawn chairs for the fireworks later. "C'mon, Miss Susan! We all sit at one big long table. The grown-ups on one end and the kids on the other."

Susan decided instantly on her strategy. "Can I sit with the kids?"

Mindy slowed down a minute to consider. "I guess you could," she said doubtfully. "Xavier likes you, and he's the biggest cousin, so he's kind of the boss."

Susan smiled at the thought of a soon-to-be-second-grader running the show. She adored Xavier, had been his first-grade teacher last year, had helped him catch up and cheered him on in his struggle with leukemia, a struggle he'd now won.

"And there's gonna be Mercedes!"

"I know! She's great." Susan was so happy for Fern and Carlo, Mercedes's foster mother and biological father, who'd fallen in love during a snowstorm over the winter and who were planning to get married soon.

"Put your stuff down here," Mindy ordered, gesturing to the promised long table on one side of the busy dining area, "and then we can go play. Look, there's Mercy!"

Susan waved at Fern, who was sitting at the table chatting with Angelica, Xavier's mom. Behind her, she heard Sam's deep voice, greeting people.

She glanced back to see that he'd paused to talk to a group of men clad in golf shirts. The preppy crowd. Of course. "I'll keep an eye on the kids," she said to Fern and Angelica, and followed the small pack of cousins before either woman could protest.

Staying with the kids would keep her from spending too much time with handsome Sam.

She watched them jump through the inflatables and play in the ball pit, all under Xavier's leadership. When he'd gotten them all onto a little train that circled the club's giant field, she sat down on a long bench under a tree to wait for the train's return.

A slight breeze rustled the leaves overhead, cooling Susan's heated face. From the bandstand, patriotic songs rang out over the chatter of families. The aroma of roasting corn and hot dogs tickled her nose, reminding her of holidays in the park in her California hometown.

Self-pity nudged at her. Holidays were meant to be experienced with family, and a lot of people here in Rescue River had a whole long tableful of relatives.

She missed her mom and brother, Aunt Sakura and Uncle Ren, and her cousins, Missy and Cameron and Ryan. They hadn't gathered often, but when they did, they'd always had a good time.

Now Uncle Ren had passed away and her cousins were scattered all over the country. She bit her lip and forced herself to concentrate on the buzz of a nearby bee, the beauty of Queen Ann's lace blooming beside the bench, the sight of Miss Lou Ann Miller carrying a tray of decorated cupcakes to the church's booth.

And of course, she wasn't alone long. No one ever was in Rescue River. There was a tap on her shoulder, and Gramps Camden, her buddy from the Senior Towers, sat down heavily beside her on the bench. With him was a weathered-looking man whom she'd occasionally seen around town but didn't know.

And that, too, never lasted long in Rescue River.

"Bob, meet Susan Hayashi. Susan, Bob Eakin. World War II Gliderman."

The thin old man held out a hand and gave her a surprisingly strong handshake. "And present-day librarian," he added with a wink. "Don't ever stop working. That's what'll kill you."

Since the man had to be in his nineties, if he'd fought in World War II, he must know what he was talking about. Susan shook his hand with both of her own. "I'm glad to meet you."

"He runs the library at the Towers," Gramps explained. "Don't worry, he was in Europe in the war, so he's not gonna have any problem with your people."

Susan smiled at the elderly man. "Thank you for your service, and I don't just mean that as a cliché," she said. "One of my great-grandfathers fought for Japan, but another was in an internment camp and eventually fought for the United States."

"Oh, in the 442nd?" His eyes lit up. "I was just reading about them. My buddy Fern brought me a new book about the various regiments."

"I can't believe you know about that! I'd love to borrow it sometime," she said. "I like history, but I don't know much about that period."

"Shame what we did to Japanese Americans back then," Mr. Eakin said. "We've learned better since. Is Rescue River treating you well?"

Susan nodded, her feeling of loneliness gone. "You're nice to ask. It's a great town. I love it here."

Gramps Camden studied her approvingly. "You fit right in. But how's your summer job with that Sam Hinton? Is he being fair to you?"

"I'm doing my best, Mr. Camden," came a deep voice behind them.

Susan spun around at the sound of it, her heart rate accelerating.

"Don't creep up on people, Hinton," Gramps

complained. "We're having a nice conversation. You just leave well enough alone."

Sam ignored the older man. "Brought you some appetizers," he said to Susan. "I didn't mean for you to get stuck watching the kids all day. Come on back and sit with the family."

Gramps snorted. "She doesn't want to listen to your dad give her the third degree, and I don't blame her."

Susan looked at Sam with alarm as she accepted the plate. "Is your dad going to give me the third degree? Why?"

"Because he's like his son," Gramps jumped in, "a millionaire with no consideration for the common folk."

Susan looked up at Sam in time to notice the hurt expression that flickered briefly across his face. Now that she knew Sam better, she understood how unfair Gramps's accusations were. Sam treated his workers well and bent over backward to contribute to the town's well-being. "Sam's not as much of a Scrooge as I expected," she told Gramps, softening her words with a smile. "Maybe your information is a little bit out of date."

"The lady's right," Bob Eakin said, elbowing Gramps Camden. "Leave the man alone.

He's done his share for Rescue River, just like we all try to do."

The kids' train returned then, and they all trooped back to the table.

Susan's plan of sitting with the children didn't hold water, though, because Helen was there and adamant about her own position as Mindy's grandmother. "I'll help her if she needs it," she insisted, sliding into the seat beside Mindy.

So Susan had to sit with the other adults. Which turned out to be okay. She stuffed herself with hamburgers and corn on the cob and potato salad, and laughed with Daisy and Angelica, and generally had a good time.

Mr. Hinton stopped by the table but demurred from eating with them. "I've got my eye on Camden. He's sitting a little too close to Lou Ann Miller, and I'd better make sure he doesn't bother her."

Daisy, Fern and Angelica exchanged glances. "Does Lou Ann have a preference for one or the other?" Daisy asked Angelica in a low voice.

"She's doing just fine on her own," Fern said. "I think she likes being single."

"Exactly," Angelica said, salting a second ear of corn. "I don't think she's wanting them to court her, but she can hardly say no if they put their plates down beside hers."

"Age cannot wither her, nor custom stale her infinite variety," quoted Fern's fiancé, Carlo, with a wink at Fern. "William Shakespeare, *Antony and Cleopatra*."

"He was in *one* play at Rescue River High School," Angelica said, rolling her eyes at her brother, "but he uses it every chance he can get. Makes him seem literary."

"I love it when you quote Shakespeare at me," Fern said, leaning her head on her husband-to-be's shoulder with an exaggerated lash-flutter.

Susan swallowed a huge bite of potato salad and waved her fork at the table of elders. "When I lived near the Senior Towers, I witnessed more drama than you see at a middle school. I wouldn't be surprised if those two came to blows over Lou Ann."

"That's for sure," Fern said with a quiet laugh. "When I go there for book group or to replenish the library cart, things can get pretty lively. Even Bob Eakin has his lady friends, and he's over ninety."

Sam was there, on the other side of Daisy, and it seemed to Susan that he watched her thoughtfully. At one point, as Angelica was apologizing for Gramps Camden's crotchety attitudes, he broke in. "I'm sorry you had to deal with all of that," he said. "I hope the older guys treated you okay."

"Mr. Eakin's going to lend me a book about Japanese who fought for the US in World War II," Susan said. "It's no problem, Sam. I always got along with older relatives."

"Maybe so, but watch out for Mr. Hinton, Senior," Angelica said in a low voice, grinning. "He's a tough nut to crack."

Another remark about Sam's dad. Hmm. After his appearance at the disastrous dinner she'd tried to cook, she wasn't looking forward to seeing him again. Although, she reminded herself, it didn't really matter what he thought. She was just a summer nanny.

Still, right at this moment, Susan felt welcomed and affirmed, almost as if she was a part of the family. Which was strange...but nice.

As they all talked about how full they were—and made trips to the buffet for seconds—a tall, curvaceous redhead walked hesitantly toward the table, her four subdued kids following, all looking to be under the age of eight.

Susan's teacher radar went up immediately.

Why weren't the kids looking happy in the presence of cotton candy and inflatables and face painters? Why the tension and caution?

Helen jumped up to greet the woman. "Fiona! Come on, right here. I have a seat for you, and we can squeeze in your little ones at this end of the table. Have you eaten?"

As she settled the woman beside Sam, Helen was practically glowing with excitement, and it all came clear to Susan.

Helen had an agenda to set Sam up with a replacement Marie. And here she was.

On Susan's other side, Daisy filled in the facts. "Fiona Farmingham. Just moved to Rescue River to escape all the gossip. Her celebrity husband just died, and it turns out he had a whole other family down in Texas."

Susan looked at the woman with sympathy. "Do the kids know?"

"Oh, yeah, they couldn't help but hear about it. Apparently, they got teased pretty bad. Fiona is Marie's distant cousin, so she knows the town. She's hoping Rescue River will be a fresh start."

"Looks like they need one."

But as sympathetic as she felt, she couldn't help feeling jealous as Sam and Fiona talked, egged on by Helen. Even after the rest of them had stood up, Sam and Fiona talked on.

Helen came over to share her triumph with Susan and Daisy. "They're hitting it off, I think," she said in a confiding voice. "Look what lovely manners she has. And she was a stay-at-home mom, and she knows just how to keep a big house nice. She was kind of Marie's role model in that."

"You doing some matchmaking, Helen?" Daisy asked bluntly.

"Sam needs a wife, and Mindy needs a mother. It should have been Marie, but since it can't…well. I hope he'll find a woman who's as like her as possible." Helen's eyes shone with unshed tears.

Susan stuffed down the feelings of hurt and inadequacy prompted by Helen's words. This was good. This was what she wanted: to keep a distance from Sam, which his serious dating of another woman would do. This would be good for Mindy, providing a mother figure and ready-made siblings.

"She's built like a model," Daisy complained in Susan's other ear. "And look, she's just picking at her food. It's hard to like a woman like that."

But Fiona soon excused herself from Sam

and came over to talk to them. "Are you guys the moms of these kids?" she asked, her voice throaty and surprisingly deep. "Because I'm fairly desperate for mom friends. I had to leave a lot of people behind when I moved, and I don't know a soul here except for Helen. Well, and I've met Mindy a time or two."

Fern, who was unfailingly kind and accepting, started chatting with Fiona about her daughter, who was the same age as Fern's daughter, Mercedes. Angelica joined in the conversation, and Susan had to admit: the woman was lovely. When she squatted down to see what the kids were doing, she greeted Mindy happily with a hug, reminding the little girl that they'd met before. Soon, she'd engaged all the kids in conversation, introducing her own, encouraging the kids to play together.

As Fiona sat back down with Sam, now surrounded by her children and Mindy, Susan ground her teeth and gave herself a firm talking to.

This was right; this was what everyone, herself included, wanted. Fiona was good with Mindy and was the type of woman Sam needed, way more than Susan herself was.

She swallowed the giant lump in her throat. She needed to leave them to it.

She excused herself from the others. She was left out anyway. Daisy had gone to see Dion and everyone else was talking. She pulled out her phone and shot Sam a text: Not feeling well, found a way home. There. That sounded breezy.

Then she slipped away and out the side door of the country club.

She'd achieved her goal of staying independent, she told herself as she started walking the two miles toward Sam's house. And it was just her own stupidity that had her feeling teary and blue about it. She'd get over it. She was meant to be alone. This was how it was to be, and it was just going to have to be good enough.

Chapter Seven

After Susan left the table, Sam tried to focus on Fiona, new in town and someone his mother-in-law wanted him to get to know better. "She's perfect for you and Mindy, Sam," Helen had whispered as Fiona approached the table. "I know, four kids is a lot, but you have the resources. And she's happy to stay at home. Wouldn't that be wonderful for Mindy?"

The hard sell had made him feel resistant, but Fiona was a genuinely nice woman. They chatted easily about the small liberal arts college they'd both attended, although in different years, about how Rescue River was a great place to raise a family, about people they knew in common, since Fiona was related to Marie.

There was something shuttered in her eyes, some distance, some pain. Still, she was pretty, with her long, wavy red hair, tall as a model but with pleasant curves. Obviously smart.

Sam's attention strayed, wondering where Susan had gone. He scanned the crowd down by the band's tent, where the sounds of pop music emerged alongside patriotic favorites. Checked the food area, where the fragrance of barbecue and burned sugar lingered.

No Susan, though.

"Look," Fiona said, "I get the sense that Helen is trying to push us together, but don't feel obligated to stick around and talk. I'm not in the market for a relationship. I'm just trying to straighten out my life after my husband's death."

He snapped back to focus on her. "I'm sorry for your loss. I faced that and I'm dealing with it, but it's not easy when you had a great relationship and high hopes for the future."

She stared off across the field where people were starting to stake out spots to watch fireworks. Craned her neck, perhaps to see her kids, who were over at the face-painting station with Mindy, under Daisy's supervision. Then she turned back to him. "Be glad if yours was a clean break, Sam," she said, her voice surprisingly intense. "Not everyone has that. In a way, it's harder if the loss was…complicated."

He cocked his head to one side, looking at her and wondering about her story.

One of her children ran to her, a girl of seven or eight, and whispered something in her ear. The two talked in low tones while Sam thought about what she had said.

Thinking about Marie.

It had, in fact, been a clean break. He'd never had any reason to doubt her faithfulness or her love. They'd been genuinely happy together. And right up to the end, her faith had been strong, had guided him even, kept him on a positive path.

It was only after her death that he'd strayed away, mentally, from his faith. Had gotten angry with God about what He'd taken away, not just from Sam himself, but from a little girl who'd sobbed for days as if her heart was breaking—which it surely was—about the loss of her loving mama.

But Mindy had only positive memories of her mother. She'd been well-cared for, and even though the loss had been terribly, terribly hard on her, she hadn't ever questioned her mother's love. She had more moments of joy than pain, these days. Nothing like the skulking, furtive demeanor of the mysterious Fiona's kids.

Marie had been everything a mother should be.

And maybe, just maybe, rather than exclusively feeling bitter about losing her, he should feel grateful to have had a faithful, loving wife.

Fiona's daughter ran off, and she turned to meet his bemused eyes.

"Are you doing okay?" he asked, feeling awkward. "Do you need someone to talk to?"

She waved a hand. "Don't worry about me. I have a strong faith and an appointment with the pastor here. I'll be fine. We'll be fine." Her face broke into a genuinely beautiful smile. "God's good even when times are hard."

"That's…true." And he wasn't just saying it. Maybe it was time for a change. Maybe he needed to not only get to church each week, but get right with God. "You've made me think," he said to Fiona. "I appreciate that."

"Sure, Sam. Nice talking to you."

The obvious ending of their conversation turned on a light bulb for him: his "find Mindy a mom" campaign was going to be harder than he thought. Because right here in front of him was a perfect woman. Exactly what he would have wanted, had he filled out an order form.

And he had zero interest in her, romantically.

She pushed back her chair, holding out a hand to briskly shake his, and he could tell she felt the same way about him, so there was no guilt. There might even be a friendship, one of these days; they seemed to have some things in common. "Your kids are welcome to swim in my pool anytime," he said. "Mindy would love the company."

"Thanks, that's nice of you." She smiled at him, but her mind was clearly elsewhere. Her eyes held pain and secrets, and Sam resolved to get Daisy on the case.

He walked around for a while, enjoying the companionship of old friends, watching the kids run around in small packs, relishing another piece of pie. But something was missing: he couldn't find Susan. Mindy was still with Daisy, who hadn't seen Susan in a while.

Finally he thought to text Susan, but when he pulled out his phone and looked at it, he saw her message.

He frowned. She'd gone home? How, when she'd ridden over with him?

Sam asked around to see whether anyone

had noticed her leaving. "I think she walked," a teenager told him offhandedly.

Walked home? That was close to three miles, mostly on deserted country roads, and darkness was falling. Not good.

He shot her a text: Where are you?

She didn't answer.

He turned to find his mother-in-law at his elbow. "How did you like Fiona?" she asked.

"Can you watch over Mindy tonight and make sure she gets home?"

"Of course!" A wide smile spread over her face. "You liked her, then? Are you taking her home?"

Had she lost her mind? Sam shook his head distractedly. "Fiona is lovely, and we have nothing going on romantically. She seems to need a friend, so if you're wanting to help her out, that's probably the direction to go. Introduce her to some of the local women, something like that."

"But if you're not going to take Fiona home," she asked unhappily, "then why are you leaving?"

"Susan walked home, and I need to check on her."

Helen put a hand on her hip, her forehead

wrinkling. "Now why would anyone do something like that? That's just strange."

He ignored the judgment. "I'll see you when you get home with Mindy," he said, turning toward the parking lot.

"But you'll miss the fireworks!" Helen sounded truly distressed. "That woman is a terrible influence on you. She's not even patriotic!"

"Later, Helen," he called over his shoulder.

After catching Mindy long enough to explain that she was to leave with her grandparents—which appeared to be fine with her, she was having such a good time with all the kids to play with—Sam got in his truck and started driving, thinking about what Helen had said.

Susan *was* different. She was independent and outspoken and didn't always say the proper thing.

But as for patriotism… Sam thought of her interactions with the older veterans and chuckled. She'd had those guys eating from the palm of her hand. She was every bit a proud American, as evidenced by the words on her obviously well-worn T-shirt.

He drove slowly along the country road, windows open. A gentle breeze brought the smells of hay and fresh-plowed soil that had always been part of his homeland experience. Crickets chirped, their music rising and falling, accompanied by a throaty chorus of frogs as he passed a small farm pond.

The sky was darkening, and up ahead, he saw the moon rise in a perfect circle, like a large round coin in the sky.

Even with the moonlight, it was still too dark. Too dark for a young woman to be out alone, a woman unfamiliar with the roads. Could Susan have gotten lost? Could something bad have happened to her?

As he arrived at Main Street in downtown Rescue River, concern grew in his heart. Where was she? Had something happened? He'd been studying the dark road the whole way and hadn't seen her, but could she have fallen into a ditch or been abducted?

Finally he spotted a petite form just sinking onto a bench, a couple of buildings down from the Chatterbox Café. Susan.

She was taking off her sandals and studying one foot, and when he stopped the truck in front of her, she looked up.

She wasn't as classically beautiful as Fiona. Her hair was coming out of its neat ponytail, and her shoulders slumped a little.

He'd never been so glad to see anyone in his life.

He jumped out of the truck and strode over to her. "What were you thinking, walking home?"

She squinted up at him. "Umm...I was tired?"

"You walked two miles on rough country roads. Of course you're tired." He sat down beside her and gestured toward the foot she'd been examining. "What happened?"

"Blister," she said. "I'll live."

He sighed and shook his head. "Wait here a minute."

He trotted over to his truck, fumbled in the glove box and returned with the small first-aid kit he always carried. "Let me see that."

"Why am I not surprised that you have a first-aid kit?" she asked, but she let him take her foot on his lap.

The skin had broken and the blister was a large, angry red. He opened an antibiotic wipe and cleansed it carefully, scolding himself internally for enjoying the opportunity to touch her delicate foot.

"Ow!" She winced when the medicine touched the broken skin.

"Sorry." He patted her ankle. "Now we'll bandage you up."

He rubbed antibiotic ointment over the hurt spot and pressed on a bandage. "There," he said. He kept a loose grip on her foot, strangely reluctant to let it go.

Without the daytime bustle, Main Street felt peaceful. The streetlights had come on. Overhead were leafy trees, and beyond them, stars were starting to blink in the graying sky.

Down the street, the lights of the Chatterbox Café clicked off.

Susan looked at him with eyes wide and vulnerable above a forced-looking smile. "Didn't you want to stay and talk with the wife Helen picked out for you?"

He felt one side of his mouth quirk up. "Was it that obvious?"

"Kinda. She seemed really nice."

"Yes, she is." He squeezed her foot a little tighter. "And no, I didn't want to stay. Not when I realized you were missing."

"I'm sorry."

"Hey." He touched her chin. "I wanted to come find you."

"How come?"

The question hung in the air between them. He looked at her lips.

Which parted a little, very prettily, and then Susan pulled her foot off his lap and twisted it around her other leg, looking nervous. "Sam…"

He brushed back a strand of hair that had tumbled down her forehead. Her skin felt soft as a baby's.

He breathed in, and leaned forward, and pressed his lips to hers.

Susan's heart pounded faster than a rock-and-roll drumbeat as Sam kissed her. Just a light brush of the lips took her breath away.

She lifted her hands, not sure whether she meant to stop him or urge him on, and her hands encountered the rough stubble on his cheek. Intrigued, she stroked his face, getting to know the planes and angles she'd been studying, without intending to, for days.

What did this mean? And why, oh why, did it have to feel so good? She drew in a sharp breath, almost a gasp, because he hadn't moved away. His handsome face was still an inch from hers, and this felt like every forbidden dream she'd ever had, coming true.

"Close your eyes," he said in his bossy way that, right now, didn't bother her in the least.

And he leaned closer and pressed his lips to hers again, just a little harder.

Susan's heart seemed to expand in her chest, reaching out toward his. Everything she'd admired about him, everything she'd been drawn to, seemed alive in the air around them.

There was a booming sound, a bunch of crackling pops, and she jerked back as Sam lifted his head. At the same time, they both realized what it was.

"Fireworks!" Sam exclaimed, a grin crossing his face. "How appropriate." He studied her tenderly. "Was that okay?"

Was it okay that he'd rocked her world? Was it okay that his lightest touch made her feel as if she was in love with him? "When I kissed my boss, I felt fireworks," she joked awkwardly to cover the tension she felt.

He looked stricken as the fireworks continued to create a display above their heads, green and red and gold. "Oh, Susan, I'm sorry."

"For what?"

"I was forgetting for a minute that you're an employee. That was completely inappropriate."

Amidst the popping and booming sounds, his words were too much to process. She was still reeling from how his kiss had made her feel, and she couldn't think why he was looking so upset.

Unless he wished he hadn't done it.

"Come on," he said, and pulled her to her feet. He didn't hold her hand, though; as soon as he was sure she was steady, he stepped a foot away. Too far! her heart called, wanting her to grab onto him. But she squashed the feelings down.

A minute later, she was in his truck and headed to his house. He drove like a silent statue, a muscle twitching in his jaw.

He pulled up in the driveway and stared straight ahead. "We'll talk tomorrow. Again, I apologize."

She looked at him, confused. Clearly she was being dismissed.

Was he angry at himself for having let his feelings go out of control? Did he even *have* feelings, or had that been just a guy thing, driven by testosterone rather than his heart?

She wanted to ask him about it, but suddenly, there was no closeness available for such a discussion.

And she was just a little too fragile to push it tonight, when her lips still tingled from his kiss, her fingertips still remembered the way his strong jaw had felt beneath them.

She'd have to face what had just happened, but not tonight.

The next morning, Sam was in his office trying to put out a few fires before his employee party when there was a hesitant knock on the door.

"Come in." He tried to ignore the way his heart leaped, but it was next to impossible. His heart knew it was Susan; Mindy wouldn't have knocked, and who else would be in the house? And his heart was very interested in being near the woman who'd kissed him back so sweetly last night.

Sure enough, it was her. Dressed in another faded red, white and blue T-shirt and short jeans and wearing a worried frown. When their eyes met, she blushed and looked away. "We have a problem."

"What's wrong?"

"I just talked to Pammy. The one who's doing the kids' entertainment for the party? Only…she can't do it."

"What do you mean?" He felt relieved that she was all business this morning. Maybe that would help his racing pulse slow down.

"They had a death in the family and they all have to rush down to West Virginia to the funeral. And since it's a family-run business, that's pretty much everyone."

He blew out a breath, thinking of all his employees with families. They looked forward to this event as a time when they could kick back and relax, bring the kids, knowing it would be fun for everyone.

"Any ideas?" he asked. Because if there was one thing he'd learned about Susan, it was that she was good in an emergency.

"As a matter of fact, yes!" A smile broke out on her face, and Sam's mouth went dry. When she was excited about something, she was pretty much irresistible.

"What's the idea?" he asked, his voice a little hoarse.

"Let's get dogs from Troy's rescue to come be the entertainment."

"No." He shook his head. "That won't work."

"Why not?"

"Dogs, instead of a clown and a dunking tank and carnival games?"

She waved a hand impatiently. "Kids like real things better than all that," she said. "If you don't believe me, ask Mindy which she'd rather see."

"Oh, I know what Mindy would choose," he said, mock-glaring at her. "She's been on me nonstop about getting a dog. It's almost like someone put her up to it." He stepped closer.

Susan's eyes darkened and her breathing quickened. "That's an argument for another day," she said primly. "And it proves my point: kids love dogs."

"It's not safe," he explained, stepping back from her dangerous appeal and half sitting on the edge of his desk. "There are liability issues. If someone got bitten, it would be on Hinton Enterprises, and bad PR as well. And more than that, I like to take care of my employees, not put them at risk."

Susan nodded, sinking down to perch on his leather client seat. "Can't we post a warning? And Troy wouldn't bring any dogs who weren't friendly."

Sam shrugged. "A warning might solve the liability issue, but…"

"But you don't like change," she said.

He opened his mouth to argue and then closed it again. "You're right, I don't. We've had Pammy do the kids' entertainment for ten years."

"But sometimes, change has to happen," she

said gently. "Pammy can't help it that she's unavailable this year. Her grandma passed."

Troy felt like a heel. "I'll send flowers," he said, making a note to himself.

"Write down, 'Puppy for Mindy's birthday,'" she suggested.

He looked up at her. She was messing with him! "Don't you ever take anything seriously?"

"Yes. Like the fact that an only child like Mindy needs a pet."

"We don't have time for a puppy."

"People manage!" She waved a hand. "There are dog walkers. Doggie day cares. Daisy was saying that new woman in town, your special friend, might start one."

"We're losing focus. Isn't there an easier way to entertain kids? You're the expert in that. Think of something!" He stood and started pacing back and forth in front of his desk, filled with restless energy.

"Yes, and I had an expert idea," she said. "The dogs. Let me go with it, Sam. It'll work great, you'll see. You won't be disappointed."

She didn't get it, how important this business, these people, were to him. How he wanted things to stay the same for them, wanted them to be safe. He stopped directly in front of her, crossing his arms. "No."

"It's community service," she teased, cocking her head to one side. "Helping animals. Doesn't that make Hinton Enterprises look good?" She edged neatly out of the chair and went around behind it, creating a barrier between them. She leaned on the back of the chair, her eyes sparkling.

He frowned away the energy her smile evoked in him. "You sure you didn't have training as a lawyer?"

"Just four or five dogs," she said, ignoring his question. "And Troy would be there the whole time."

Sam felt as if he was losing a business negotiation, which never happened. But then again, he never sat across the table from a negotiator like Susan.

She raised an eyebrow at him. "Embrace the change, Sam. Sometimes, it can be a good thing."

He sighed. "If Troy can be there the whole time," he said grudgingly, "I guess we can give it a try."

Chapter Eight

Susan slipped out midmorning and power-walked to the park in downtown Rescue River. Hopefully, the materials to set up for Sam's work picnic would be here. Hopefully, Daisy would be, too, to help her.

Hopefully, Sam wouldn't be anywhere nearby.

She didn't need the distraction of her boss, kisser *extraordinaire*.

Last night had been amazing, wonderful. Her heart, which she kept so carefully guarded beneath her mouthy exterior, had shown itself to be the marshmallow that it was and melted.

And as a result, Sam's coldness and dismissal afterward had bludgeoned said heart.

Back to the old way, the independent way. She'd decided it last night, and kept herself busy putting out fires and getting the new kids' entertainment organized this morning. Their little argument had fanned the attraction flames a bit, but she'd stayed businesslike and she was proud of it.

As she got to the park, she was glad to see that the large tent was up and the tables there. Sam spared no expense for his workers, but at the same time, he didn't want it to be overly fancy. He just wanted everyone to feel comfortable and have fun. So her job was to add a touch of down home to the whole thing.

"Hey!" Daisy strolled toward her, yawning. "Where's the coffee?"

Knowing her friend, Susan had stopped at the Chatterbox and picked up two cups. "Here's yours, black with sweetener." She handed it over.

Daisy sank down on a bench beside the tent while Susan opened all the boxes.

"Here's our centerpieces," Susan said, holding up a bunch of kids' tractors. "Sam had me order enough so that every kid can take one home. We'll march them along the green runners so it looks like they're, you know, on a farm."

"Sweet." Daisy took a long drink of coffee. And it *was* sweet. Sam was good to his employees. An amazing boss, an amazing man. A real catch.

Just not for her.

To distract herself from the sudden ache in her heart, Susan looked around. There was a father and son tossing a softball while a nearby mom spread a red-and-white plastic tablecloth over the picnic table. At one of the park's pavilions, two pregnant women sprawled on benches while their husbands fired up the park's grills and a couple of babies played at their feet.

And there was Fiona, the new mom in town, pushing her youngest on the swings while her other three children kicked a ball nearby.

Susan had talked to her mom this morning. Apparently Donny was doing well at camp, but her mom sounded not so great. Surprisingly lonely. She'd even asked about how Susan was doing and how she liked her new job, whether she needed anything. It was an uncharacteristically maternal call, and Susan wondered what was going on with her mother.

Thinking about her family made her miss them. Susan sighed. "Holidays can be hard for us single folks."

Daisy didn't answer, and when Susan glanced

over, she saw that her friend's eyes were filled with tears.

"What's wrong, honey?" Susan asked, sinking down onto the bench beside her.

Daisy shook her head. "I'm so tired of being single, but I just can't get into dating."

"Not even Dion?"

Daisy stared at her as if she'd grown two heads. "No!"

"Why not?"

"We're friends. I don't want to mess up a good friendship by trying to go romantic."

"But friendship is a good basis—"

"No way."

"Keep praying about it," Susan said, because obviously her friend wasn't open to discussing the topic further, "and I will, too."

"Pray about yourself while you're at it," Daisy advised, "because you and Sam have some major vibes going on between you."

Heat climbed into Susan's cheeks. "It's obvious?"

"To me, it is, because I know both of you so well," Daisy said. "What's going on between the two of you, anyway?"

Susan contemplated telling her best friend about the kiss. For about ten seconds. But Daisy was protective of her brother and Susan wasn't at all sure about how she felt about it, so she clamped her jaw shut and got busy unpacking tractor centerpieces.

"Susan? Are you seriously not going to answer?"

"Nothing's going on," Susan said firmly.

A welcome distraction came in the form of Xavier, who jumped into Daisy's lap. A minute later, Angelica appeared with baby Emmie in her arms, breathless. "Hey guys," she said.

"Where's Mindy?" Xavier asked.

"She'll be here soon, with her dad. Which makes me think we'd better get more done."

"Oh, Sam will be worrying, all right," Daisy said.

"Hey," Angelica said. "Is Mindy all set for camp?"

"I think so," Susan said. "It's next weekend, right?"

"That's right," Angelica said, "but when I mentioned it to Sam, he didn't seem to know anything about it."

"I told him," Susan said. "He wrote the check. I'll talk to him about it." But uneasiness clenched her stomach. The camp was one Xavier was attending for a week, with Angelica, and they had a special program where younger siblings and relatives could come for a weekend. She and Angelica had discussed it, and while she'd explained the details to Sam, he'd been distracted. She'd been surprised when he said it was okay.

Hopefully, this was just a little misunderstanding she could clear up quickly when he arrived, and then she could fade into the background and refill bowls of potato chips and play with Mindy.

They soon had the tent decorated in patriotic, farm decor. Just in time, because the caterers arrived to put out the food, all-American hot dogs and hamburgers, plus a taco bar and tamales.

She and Daisy sank down at a picnic table with cold drinks.

"I'm sweating already," Daisy said.

"Me, too." Susan fanned herself with a napkin.

"Any thoughts of getting work done?" came a stern voice behind them.

The hairs on Susan's arms stood on end. Sam.

Daisy raised her eyebrows at Susan, ignoring her brother. "Somebody's cranky. Wonder what's wrong with him?"

He kissed me and he regrets it. Susan shrugged. "Who knows?"

Mindy, who'd come with Sam but stopped at the swings where Xavier was, ran up to them. "Daddy, Xavier says I can ride with them to camp. And I'm going to stay in a tent!"

Sam looked down at her and then his face focused. "Camp? What camp?"

Mindy looked worriedly at Susan. "I'm going to that camp with Xavier. Right?"

"Right," she said reassuringly, and turned to Sam. Best to get this over with now. "It's that special-needs camp. Xavier goes every summer, as a cancer survivor. They have a program for kids with limb differences. We talked about this."

"No, we didn't. When is it and where?"

"It's next weekend, or at least, Mindy's part is only for the weekend. In West Virginia."

Sam's eyes widened. "She's not going to sleepaway camp in West Virginia. She's five!"

"Daddy! I'm almost six!" Mindy drew a big six in the air to make sure everyone understood.

Susan squatted down. "I'll explain it all to Daddy. You run and keep Xavier company, okay?"

"Okay," Mindy said doubtfully, and ran off.

Sam's face was tight and closed as she led him over to a quieter part of the park.

"We talked about this. It's a done deal." Even as she spoke, guilt clutched at her. Sam had been distracted with Helen's arrival, the evening after they'd gone to the lake. He'd gotten a phone call when she'd been explaining the details, and he'd signed the check amidst a lot of other household expenses.

He shook his head. "I didn't okay her sleeping away. She's way too young."

"They have programs for younger kids who go with relatives. Angelica's going." She paused for emphasis. "Sam, I think it'll be good for her. She needs to meet other kids with limb differences."

"No."

Susan drew in her breath and counted to ten. "She's going to be very disappointed. She wants to go with Xavier. And Angelica will be there the whole time."

"Parents can go?"

She nodded, knowing exactly what he would say.

"Then I'll go."

"Sam." She touched his arm. "Troy and Angelica think it'll be best if you don't go."

"Troy and Angelica aren't Mindy's parents. And neither are you."

That truth hit her like a whip to the heart.

She needed to watch herself, because her feelings as Mindy's nanny had begun to overflow their professional boundaries. It was all too easy to love the little girl. Easy to care too much about Mindy's dad, too, who was currently glaring at her, intent on putting her in her place.

She swallowed her hurt feelings. "I know that! I'm just someone who cares about her and has a role taking care of her. And who knows what kids with special needs, need."

He glared. "If I'm not going, then Mindy can't, either."

She threw up her hands, exasperated. "Fine. It's your money you're wasting. And it's you who can explain to Mindy why she can't go. I'm going to..." She looked around. "Set up the salt and pepper shakers at a perfect angle because I'm sure the control-freak boss of Hinton Enterprises will come in and redo it if I don't."

She spun and stormed into the tent.

Soon Sam was back in charming boss mode, and Susan watched him and marveled at his self-control. He'd been furious at her five minutes ago, but now he was all professional.

And it was clear his employees loved him. They crowded around him, and teased, but with respect; they listened to everything he had to say.

There was a moment when she thought the dog thing was going to be a disaster. Just when he'd stood to make his traditional speech, a squirrel had run past the dog crates and the dogs had gone haywire with barking, drowning out whatever Sam was saying.

But Sam responded graciously, with a joke, while Troy got the dogs under control, and then Sam continued his speech without a hitch.

Several people expressed interest in adopting dogs. And the local paper had come to cover the event and snapped more pictures of the dogs than anything else. Undoubtedly, there'd be a feel-good story featuring Hinton Enterprises in the paper tomorrow.

The downside, if you were looking at it from Sam's point of view, was that Mindy fell in love with a little black-and-white mutt with a bandage on one leg. While Mindy cradled it, Troy explained to Sam how it was non-shedding and, at three years old, already house-trained. "It'll probably always have a limp, though," Troy had said.

"It's got a hurt paw, like me," Mindy had said, cuddling the dog.

Susan's heart squeezed, and she looked up at

Sam. The raw love for his little girl that shone out of his eyes almost hurt. She had a feeling that Mindy would end up with that little dog as a birthday present.

As the party went on, Sam seemed to let go of control a little bit and relax. The children played with the dogs and enjoyed the park and the play equipment, running hard, making up games. That gave the adults space to linger over their plates of food, talking and laughing. Aside from a few teenagers, no one seemed to have their cell phones out.

It was an old-fashioned type of picnic that could have just as easily taken place fifty years ago. A perfect kind of event for an old-fashioned, close-knit community like Rescue River, and Susan was proud of her part in organizing it.

Until the topic of Sam's being single came up. "We think Mr. Hinton needs a girlfriend," said Eduardo, a good-looking, thirtysomething groundsman at Hinton Enterprises. He sometimes moonlighted for Sam, helping with the landscaping around the house, and seemed to hold a privileged position among the Hinton workers; right now, he was sitting at a table with Sam and five or six other employees.

Sam's father, who'd been sitting at an adjoining table with Susan and Daisy, spoke up.

"That's exactly what he needs. But not just a girlfriend, a wife."

"And a mama for his little girl," one of the older secretaries said.

"Hey, what about Susan?" someone said, and the group at the picnic table turned to look at her. "She's single, and she already takes care of Mindy."

"Good call," Eduardo said. *"Muy bonita."*

Totally mortified, Susan stared at the ground. She knew she should come up with some kind of a joke to make the moment go by easily, but for the life of her, she couldn't think of one.

"You people need to stick to business, and so do I." Sam's voice was strained.

"But Daddy," Mindy chimed in, climbing up into Sam's lap, "I *do* want a mommy!"

The images evoked by those sweet words made Susan's cheeks flame and her heart ache with longing. To be wanted, needed, cherished. To finally have a real home.

She stole a glance at Sam's clenched jaw. Obviously, his employees' suggestions hadn't induced the same images and longings in him. And he wasn't finding the gentle jokes funny, either.

If only the ground would open up and swallow her.

* * *

Sam stood under a giant oak tree in the Rescue River Park, talking to a group of five or six longtime employees who didn't seem to want to leave.

Even while he listened and laughed with them, he couldn't help watching Susan.

Apparently, she'd recovered just fine from that awkward moment with his employees. She was tying garbage bags and helping to carry heavy food trays to the truck. When a little boy ran up crying, she squatted down to listen, then took his hand and walked back to the tent to find the tractor he'd left on a table.

As he watched, Eduardo approached her, spoke for a minute, then gave her a friendly handshake that, to Sam's eyes, went on a little bit too long and was accompanied by a little too much eye contact.

He tamped the jealousy down. He didn't want Susan as a long-term part of his life, so why feel bad when other men admired her? She was totally inappropriate for him. Just witness this whole ridiculous camp situation. His blood pressure rose just thinking of Mindy going to camp.

Marie would never have allowed it.

But Marie's gone, and you have to move on.

That new voice inside him was unfamiliar and unwelcome, but Sam was honest enough to know that it spoke truth. He had to stop focusing on Marie, had to let her go.

But if he did that, would his life be as it had been for the past twenty-four hours—crazy and emotional? Going from the intense excitement of kissing Susan to the low of feeling guilty, like a bad boss hitting on his employee? Angry about the camp. Embarrassed by his workers' jokes.

He didn't want such an exciting life, couldn't handle it. He wanted life on an even keel. Stable. Comfortable.

As he bid goodbye to the final couple of workers, his father approached. He'd stayed in the background during the picnic, letting Sam have center stage, but Sam had been conscious of him, as always. Though his father's health didn't permit him to run Hinton Enterprises anymore, he'd started the company and cared about its success, and Sam always respected his opinions.

"What did you think?" he asked his dad.

His father clapped him on the back. "Another good picnic," he said. "You have a way with the workers. They like you."

"Thanks." He knew what his father wasn't

saying; the workers liked Sam better than they'd liked his father. Personality difference, and maybe the struggles of starting something from the ground up. His father wasn't an easy man to get along with.

Sam knew he wasn't always easy, either, but he at least could laugh at himself—usually— and listen to other people's ideas, talents his father had never mastered.

Since his father was so hard to please, his approving remarks about the event felt good.

They turned together to stroll back toward the almost-empty tent. Just in time to see Mindy run to Susan, hug her legs and get lifted into her arms.

"Looks like those two are close," Mr. Hinton remarked.

Sam nodded slowly. "It sure does."

"You worried about that?" Mr. Hinton asked.

"A little," Sam admitted. "But Mindy needs women in her life. She's attached to Daisy, and now to Angelica, but those two aren't always around. Susan fills in the gaps, that's all."

"Are you sure that's all?" His father's thick eyebrows came together, and though he was a good head shorter than Sam, his expression was enough to make Sam feel ashamed, as if his father had seen that moment under the street lamp.

"It has to be," he said. "Things couldn't work between us."

Mr. Hinton nodded, looking relieved. "I didn't think she was your type, but I was starting to wonder. Figured you'd do the right thing." He shook his head. "Back in my day, races didn't mix. Oh, we always had a lot of different colors in Rescue River, but for marrying, they stuck to themselves. Times might be changing, but it's hard for me to keep up."

"Dad," Sam said automatically. "What a person looks like doesn't matter, you know that. We're all of the same value to God."

His father frowned at him. "Never thought to hear you spouting religion at me."

Sam laughed. "Surprise myself sometimes," he said.

As his father walked off, Sam sank down on a park bench rather than interrupting the moment between Mindy and Susan. He needed to think.

He probably needed to pray, too, but this wasn't the time or the place.

Still, under the stars, he thought about his goal of finding a mother for Mindy and made a decision.

He wouldn't try so hard to replace Marie anymore. It wasn't working, and it wasn't possible.

But a woman like Susan wasn't possible, either. He wasn't the man to handle it.

Instead, he'd focus on being the best single dad he could be.

People did that. Look at his employee, Eduardo; he'd been a single parent for years. And several other dads at Mindy's school were going it alone.

Anyway, Susan was way too young for him.

He'd go forward single and let Mindy's nurturing needs be filled by his female relatives, by teachers, by the church.

It wasn't what Marie had wanted, and looking up into the starry sky, he shot an apology her way. "I'm sorry, Marie," he whispered. "I don't think I can keep my promise, at least not right now."

He let out a huge sigh as sadness overwhelmed him.

The quest to remarry had helped him get by, had given him a goal. Without it, emptiness and loneliness pushed at him like waves lapping the shore.

He had to find his center again, his stability. Had to get right with God. Had to learn to go on alone.

It was the only thing he could do, but it didn't feel good. Just for a minute, he let his head sink down into his hands and mourned the loss of a dream.

The next morning, Sam broke all of his own Sunday morning rules, flipping on a mindless TV show for Mindy and handing her a donut. Then he ushered Susan into his office.

She was wearing close-fitting black pants and a jade-green sleeveless shirt that showed off her tanned, shapely arms. Jade earrings swung from her ears, giving her a carefree vibe. But her expression was closed tight.

During the night, he'd gotten over some of his anger about the camp situation. He probably hadn't listened carefully enough to what she'd been telling him. Half the time, when Susan talked to him, he got caught up in her honeysuckle perfume and her shiny hair and her lively, sparkling dark eyes; it wasn't surprising that he might have missed some of the details she'd shared with him.

Now that he'd made a new commitment to staying single, maybe he could pay more attention to what she had to say.

And today, he just had to keep a cool, professional distance, make her see reason and get her on his side, so that she could help him explain to Mindy that she wouldn't be going to camp.

"Sit down," he said, ushering her to the same chair she'd sat in the day he'd interviewed her. Thinking of that day almost made him chuckle. When he'd suspected she'd be a handful to work with, he hadn't been wrong.

She perched warily on the edge of the seat. "We only have half an hour before we should leave for church," she said. "Or at least, I'm going to church. Are you?"

He nodded. "There'll be time. He spread his hands and gave her a friendly-but-impersonal smile. "I guess when I agreed to Mindy going to camp, I wasn't really listening," he said. "I'm sorry about that, but I really do think she's too young to go."

Susan nodded, and for the first time he noticed that there were dark circles under her eyes. "I lay awake thinking about it, and I want you to know I feel bad about what happened. I should have made sure I had your full attention about such an important decision."

Relief washed over him. This wasn't going

to be as hard as he'd feared. "I'm glad you see it my way."

"Well, but I don't exactly see it your way," she said, flashing a smile at him. "You were wrong, too, not to pay attention about your child's summer plans. Now Mindy has a spot at the camp and some other child doesn't. It wouldn't be right to back out."

He hadn't thought of that. "I'll pay for the place," he said, waving his hand in an effort to dismiss her concern. Wanting to dismiss it himself, and not quite succeeding.

"It's not just that, Sam," she said quietly. "Mindy needs this camp. She needs to go where other kids with limb differences are. She needs to see what's possible for her and what's positive. For example, why doesn't she have an artificial limb?"

"We tried that when she was little. She hated it."

"From what I've read, that's common," she said. "But now that she's a little older, she might want one. And I'm sure the technology has advanced. It's something she can learn about at the camp, get a feel for it, see some kids with artificial limbs and others managing without."

He had to admit, Susan had a point. "In that case, maybe she should go. And—" he said to cut off Susan's expression of victory. "I should go, too."

She bit her lip and shook her head, looking regretful. "I thought of that. I mean, of getting you a space there, too. The problem is that the camp is entirely full. There are no more spaces for adults. I checked online last night, and they texted me a confirmation this morning. No more space."

He frowned. "Then she can't go."

"Sam." Susan leaned forward. "Why don't you want her to, really?"

The question floated in the air.

"I wish you hadn't talked to her about it so much," he heard himself blustering, knowing he was avoiding giving her an answer.

She nodded slowly. "I'm sorry. I should have made sure you understood what you were signing." Her voice was contrite. "And the last thing I want to do is cause Mindy to be disappointed. I…I really have no vested interest in this happening, Sam. For what mistakes I've made, I apologize."

Her accepting responsibility took the wind out of his sails. "I made mistakes, too," he said grudgingly. "I get too caught up in my work and don't pay attention to other people enough. You're…not the first person who's told me that."

"Anyone can get distracted," she said with a shrug. "So you're not perfect."

"That's it?" he asked. "You're not going to yell at me?"

She looked amused. "No. Should I?"

He settled back and stared at her, then down at his desk. That was new to him. Susan admitted her own mistakes, and she accepted that he made mistakes, too.

Hashing things out with someone like Susan, openly flawed, was actually a little more comfortable than arguing with someone practically perfect, like Marie.

Guilt washed over him. The very thought that there was something as good as, even better than, being with Marie seemed disloyal.

"Hey." Susan grabbed an old ruler that was sitting on the edge of his desk and gave his hand a light, playful whack. "What's going on in there? You never answered my question. Why are you so afraid to let Mindy go to camp with her aunt and cousin?"

He grabbed the ruler, pointed it at her and met her eyes. "I do have my reasons, young lady."

She lifted an eyebrow, waiting.

"The main reason is…" He started, then paused.

"Spill it."

He looked out the window, watching the leaves rustle in the slight breeze. "The main reason is that I don't like her to be so far out of my sight."

"Out of your control, hmm?" She was laughing at him. "Get used to it, Dad. She's growing up."

He smiled ruefully. "I'm not ready for that."

"Are you really going to be so lonely?" she asked in a teasing voice. "If it's too much to face alone, I can keep you company."

"Oh, is that so?" His whole body felt sharp with interest and surprise and…something else.

A pretty pink blush flamed across her cheeks. She picked up his tape holder and studied it with intense interest.

His hand shot out to cover hers. "A date? Maybe at Chez La Ferme?"

She dropped the tape holder and tried to pull her hand back, but he held on until she met his eyes.

"Are you asking me out?"

"Would you go?"

Their eyes met and held. Their hands were pressed together, too, and it didn't seem like either of them was breathing.

Then she pulled back and looked away, and he let her go.

"Now it's you who hasn't answered my question," he said, barely recognizing his own throaty voice. "Will you go out with me?"

"I don't… I don't know."

He leaned forward, not sure if he should press his advantage or retract the question. He knew what he *wanted* to do, but was it the right thing? "I shouldn't be asking you out when you're an employee. I don't mean to put any pressure on you, at all. You have your job whether you say yes or no. Nothing would change."

Her dark eyes flashed up to meet him. "Thanks for that," she said. "I appreciate your being so careful, considering that I'm just a temporary nanny. And…well, it's true that I don't have plans for the weekend."

Triumph surged through him, but he tamped it down.

"And I've never actually eaten at Chez La Ferme."

"So what you're saying is…" He prompted.

"Yes," she said, her voice a little bit breathy. "Yes, I'll go out with you."

And she stood, spun and hurried out of the room, leaving Sam to wonder what on earth he'd been thinking to ask Susan out.

Chapter Nine

The next Friday afternoon, Susan climbed the stairs to her over-the-garage apartment, arguing with Daisy the whole way. Quiet Fern was following along, shaking her head.

"It doesn't make sense for me to get all dressed up. This is Sam! He's seen me in my sweats, in my ratty jeans, without makeup…"

"But you're going to Chez La Ferme," Fern said hesitantly. "That's super dressy, right?"

"Exactly!" Daisy said, her voice triumphant. "You can't wear ratty jeans to Chez La Ferme."

"They fired me once, what more can they do to me?" Susan asked as she opened the door. "Come on in. Not like I have a choice about it."

"I'm sorry, Susan," Fern said, looking stricken. "If you don't want us here…"

"Fern. You're fine. It's *her* I don't want."

Susan flung an arm toward her best friend. "Because she's got some kind of an agenda that I don't share."

Daisy ignored her, walked over to the refrigerator and pulled out sodas.

"Make yourself at home, why don't you?" Susan said sarcastically. But the truth was, she was glad to have the other two women around. She was way too antsy about her date with Sam tonight.

Why had she offered to keep him company? Why had he jumped on the idea and upped the ante to a real date at Chez La Ferme? Maybe it was just something to do, and after all, he did sort of own the restaurant. Maybe this was all just business.

She'd run into Daisy at the library and made the mistake of confiding the reason for her anxiety. Daisy had taken one look at her and insisted on coming back to help her get dressed. Since Fern was leaving work at the same time, they'd talked her into coming along.

Now, Susan tore open a bag of BBQ potato chips and started pouring them into a bowl, only to have Daisy snatch the bag away. "No. Uh-uh. You're not eating those and then going on a date."

"Why not?" Susan asked.

Daisy and Fern looked at each other and burst out laughing.

"What?" Susan looked from one to the other.

"It's just," Fern said, still chuckling, "if you would happen to get close enough to kiss…"

"Your breath would reek like a third grader's," Daisy finished.

"We're not getting close enough to kiss," Susan said as heat climbed up her face.

"Here." Daisy found a bag of pretzels and tossed it to her. "Have these instead. Fern and I will eat the stinky chips."

"Well, actually," Fern said, blushing, "I think I'll stick to pretzels, too."

Daisy's eyebrows shot up. "Plans with Carlo tonight?"

"We like to watch movies on Friday nights, and it's my turn to pick."

"What are you watching?"

Fern grinned. "*Casablanca*. What's not to like? There's manly war drama for Carlo and romance for me."

"Fine," Daisy said, grabbing the bag of chips. "So I'm the only one without plans. I get the whole bag. Now, what are you wearing tonight?"

"I don't know." Susan looked at the pretzels but had no appetite. She took a sip of diet soda instead. "I have, like, one fancy dress, and I haven't worn it in a year at least. I don't know if it even fits."

"Let's see it," Daisy ordered.

Susan walked back to her bedroom and pulled out the turquoise silk. With a mandarin collar and buttons up the front, it fit snugly and had a perfectly modest hemline...until you noticed the slit that revealed a little leg.

But was that too dressy? This was Sam. She rummaged in her closet and pulled out a plain black skirt. She carried both garments out. "I'm thinking the skirt," she said.

Both Fern and Daisy said "no" at the same time.

"Wear the blue one," Daisy ordered.

"It's gorgeous," Fern agreed.

"But it's Sam, and it's Rescue River. Won't I feel way out of place?"

"You used to work at Chez La Ferme, right? Don't people dress up to go there?"

Susan thought back and nodded, reluctantly. Even Miss Minnie Falcon had worn a beaded dress when she'd come to the restaurant, and most of the men wore suits.

"What's Sam wearing?" Fern asked.

Susan shrugged. "I don't know." Truthfully, they hadn't seen much of each other since that weighted conversation that had led to this date. She wouldn't have thought they were on, except he'd sent her a text message confirming the time. And he'd washed his sleek black sports car and parked it in the driveway, so evidently they weren't going in her car. As if, Susan thought, giggling a little hysterically.

"I'll text him," Daisy offered.

"No!" Susan grabbed for her phone.

"Why not?"

"I don't want him to think I care what we wear!"

"Because…"

"Because I don't want it to seem like a real date!" Her voice broke on the last word and she sank down onto the couch, focusing on pinching a thread off the blue dress while she pulled herself together.

"Hey," Daisy said, coming to sit next to her. "You sound really upset. What's wrong?"

Susan swallowed the lump in her throat. "My dad sent me this dress because he said I had nothing decent to wear on dates with a real good prospect. So that's where I did wear it: on dates with my ex-fiancé."

"Oh." Daisy nodded.

"You were engaged?" Fern asked, her voice sympathetic.

Susan waved her hand impatiently. "Ancient history. It didn't work out because he wanted a dishrag of a wife. Like all businesspeople." She shot a glare at Daisy. "Like Sam, so don't go matching me up permanently with him."

"Who said anything about that?"

"Nobody!" Heat clamped into Susan's cheeks. Nobody had said anything about a permanent connection between her and Sam, so why had she mentioned it? What was she thinking?

"Don't you want to get married someday?" Fern asked quietly.

"No!" Susan said. "Marriage sucks the life out of women."

"It doesn't have to," Fern said. "I'm really looking forward to marrying Carlo."

Way to put your foot in your mouth, Susan. "I'm just going on my mom's example. I'm sorry," Susan apologized. "What you and Carlo have seems wonderful. But for me...for women in my family...marriage is the path to destruction."

"Nothing like being melodramatic," Daisy said, looking up from her phone.

"I'm not being melodramatic. I'm afraid I'll lose myself and then he'll leave! Just like what happened to my mom."

The comment hung in the air.

"Oooh," Fern said. "That does sound scary."

Daisy shook her head. "The past doesn't have to repeat itself. You're a completely different woman from your mom." Her phone buzzed and she glanced down at it. "Sam's wearing a suit, by the way."

"You asked him?" Susan practically shouted.

"So you should wear the blue dress. Go put it on, since you're not going to eat."

Susan drew in her breath and let it out in a sigh, then did what her friend said.

Buttoning the cuffs of a new dress shirt—cuff links would probably be excessive for a woman like Susan—Sam looked in the mirror and thought of his teary departure from Mindy just a few hours ago.

Oh, Angelica had comforted her, all too well. It made him realize how much Mindy needed a female figure in her life. And while he wanted to go forward with his plan to be single, this whole camp thing had put him back in doubt. Mindy needed a mom.

And there was the additional question: with Mindy gone, what was he supposed to do with himself this weekend? He didn't even get to go pick Mindy up because Troy was going to the camp to visit Xavier and had offered to bring Mindy home.

I'll keep you company, Susan had said in her throaty voice. He used water to tame his unruly hair and then decided he should shave after all, and took off the shirt so he wouldn't get anything on it. Man, he was acting like a teenager. He'd been on so many dates. Why was this one such a big deal?

Because it's Susan.

Susan, who was completely inappropriate for him. Susan, who wouldn't fall into line easily with any of his plans, for Mindy or otherwise. Susan, who was way too full of opinions and ideas of her own.

Susan, whose hair was like silk and whose laughter was like jazz music, rich and complex.

Susan, the very thought of whom made his heart rate speed up.

He had it bad.

Susan sat back in her soft and comfortable chair at Chez La Ferme. "You really want to hear that story?" she asked.

"I'm curious why your engagement ended, but if you don't want to talk about it, it's okay. I want this evening to be fun for you, not bringing up unpleasant memories."

"No, it's okay." Susan was surprised at how comfortable she felt. Oh, there'd been a few awkward moments at first, like when he'd come to her door. She'd seen Sam in a suit before, but tonight, knowing he'd dressed up for her, she found him devastatingly handsome.

And when he'd seen her, he'd offered a simple "You look great," but the way his eyes had darkened had sent the heat rushing to her cheeks.

Men didn't usually look at her that way, as if she was gorgeous. It took some getting used to, but...she *could* get used to it. Could learn to love it.

Even so, she'd gone into the meal with her guard up, determined to keep her distance. But Sam, with his pleasant, non-threatening conversation, gentle questions and self-deprecating jokes, had ruthlessly displayed his charm, causing her to drop that guard right back down.

"So, your engagement?" he prompted.

She'd keep it light, in line with the rest of the evening. "We actually broke up in Infinite. That super-exclusive department store in LA?"

He looked surprised. "I'm familiar with it."

"Well then, you can imagine the scene. Frank, his mother, the high-powered registry consultant and me, in their bridal registry salon." She squirmed, remembering. "Not my kind of place."

"You seem more the casual type."

"Exactly. But he and his mom and the consultant were trying to get me to register for formal china and super-expensive linens, stuff none of my friends could afford." She shook her head. "I saw my mom's life flashing before my eyes, you know? Trying to live up to somebody else's dream, trying to make a man happy when he couldn't be pleased."

He nodded, actually seeming interested in her rambling story. "What did you do?"

"Well, I...I'd read about how you can just have charitable donations at your wedding instead of gifts."

"That's usually something older couples do, right? People that already have what they need to set up housekeeping?"

She shrugged. "We had what we needed. Especially compared to the kids who could benefit from donations to Children International, which is the group I decided I wanted our guests to donate to. Frank made plenty of money."

"Okay..."

"So I...kind of stood up and said we were

done at Infinite, that we weren't going to do a bridal registry after all."

He arched an eyebrow. "I guess that didn't go over well."

"It didn't." She reflected back on the scene, the horror on the saleswoman's face, the identical disapproval on Frank's and his mother's. "It wasn't that they didn't like charity, it was that such things weren't done among their friends. We ended up yelling—well, I did—and I got kicked out of Infinite, and Frank was totally embarrassed, and then he didn't want to marry me anymore."

"And were you heartbroken?" he asked, the tiniest twinkle in his eye.

"No." She'd been hurt, of course, and her mother had been furious, but mostly, she'd felt relieved. "It made me realize how different we were, and that I could never have made him happy." And she was done talking about it and wanted to change the subject. "I ate too much tonight. That was really good."

He waved for the check and smiled at her. "I overdid it, too. Maybe we need a walk?"

"Sure."

"Was everything okay, you guys?" Tawny, their server, asked as she handed Sam the check. "It's so great to see you guys here! I can't get over it. And I'm learning how to stand up for myself better, Susan. What you did to that one jerk really made a difference to me."

Sam's pen, signing the check, slowed down, and he glanced up at Susan and raised an eyebrow.

She felt herself blushing. "I'm glad," she said, smiling at the girl, who did seem a little more mature than at the beginning of the summer. "You did a good job tonight. You're a better waitress than I'll ever be."

"Aw, thank you!"

Tawny hurried away as Max, the restaurant owner and Susan's former boss, approached their table. "I trust everything was satisfactory, Mr. Hinton?"

He looked up, winked at her. "Ask the lady."

Which put her former boss in the position of having to treat her as a valued customer. Ha! It felt so gratifying that she had to be gracious about it. "It was fantastic, Max. And it's a lot easier from this side of the table. Tawny's a good waitress."

After another minute of small talk, Sam made some subtle sign of dismissal and turned to Susan. "Ready for a walk?" he asked with just the faintest hint of wolfishness.

Suddenly, she wasn't sure, but she didn't want to let her nerves show. "Sounds good."

He held her elbow as she stood and helped her drape her lacy shawl around her shoulders. "How are your shoes?" he asked, looking down.

She held one out for him to see and was glad she'd painted her toenails to match her dress. "Wedges. Very comfortable."

"Good." He ushered her out of the restaurant with a hand on her back, nodding to a couple of patrons.

"You know," she said as soon as they were out in the parking lot, "we might've just started a whole lot of gossip."

"I didn't see Miss Minnie Falcon," Sam said with a smile.

"No, but that lady with the white updo? That's one of Miss Minnie's best friends. She'll describe us, and the news will be all over the Senior Towers." She frowned. "Not to mention that Tawny's a talker."

"You think people are that interested?"

"In you, yes. Everyone cares about who the local millionaire takes to dinner." By unspoken agreement, they'd started strolling away from town, down a dirt road between two fields, one planted with corn and one with soybeans. The rural fragrances blew on a warm breeze, pungent.

"I've taken a good number of guests to dinner there," Sam said. "It shouldn't be that noteworthy."

"Good to know I'm part of a crowd." She meant the remark to be a joke, but it came out sounding hurt.

He heard it, clearly, and put an arm around her shoulders. "I can truthfully say I've never had more fun." He squeezed her to his side. "You're a great conversationalist. I really like being with you."

"Thanks." Timidly, she put an arm around his waist, and her heart rate shot into the stratosphere, so she let it drop, pretending she'd just meant a quick hug. "I had a good time, too." She hesitated, then added, "I'm glad we're friends."

He turned to face her and took her hands in his. "Is that what we are, Susan? Friends?"

She looked up at him, noticing the way the moonlight highlighted the planes of his face. "Aren't we?"

He drew in a breath. "I'm…trying to figure that out." He looked to the side, across the cornfield, for a long moment and then looked back at her. "The thing is, I can't seem to get around this feeling I have for you. I've tried. I've told myself we're opposites, that it wouldn't work. I've tried to connect with women who are more my type. But it's not working, and I've got to admit to myself…" He leaned in. "I've got to admit, I'm falling in love with you."

Susan's heart fluttered madly, like a caged songbird, and she couldn't seem to catch her breath. This was the moment she'd never thought to have. Shouldn't she be thrilled? Why did she feel so confused?

She replayed what he'd said in her mind.

"I know you're your own woman and think your own way," he went on, "but I'm wondering if you might put some of that aside for Mindy and me."

The mention of Mindy pushed Susan's questions away for a minute. Mindy was a wonderful little girl, so easy to love.

But Sam… She looked up at him, biting her lip.

His smile told her he already knew what her reaction would be.

Because after all, when did the poor teacher from a messed-up family say no to the handsome millionaire?

He leaned down as if he was going to kiss

her, and she took a giant step back. Back from him, and back from the confusion he was causing her.

Having her hands free from his felt better. Safer. She propped one on her hip. "So you overcame your scruples and fell in love against your better judgment? And I'm supposed to be grateful, and give up being my own woman, and put my own needs and plans aside?"

"I didn't mean it that way." Behind him, clouds skittered across the moon.

Her heart was still pounding, almost as if she was afraid. But she wasn't afraid, was she? She was angry. "Haven't you ever read *Pride and Prejudice*?"

Her tone pushed the romantic expression from his eyes. "No."

"Well, if you had, you'd know that this type of a declaration leaves a little bit to be desired," she snapped.

He shook his head as if to clear it. "Wait. I did something wrong, and I have no idea what it is."

"Seriously, Sam?" She put her hands on her hips. "You practically told me how bad you feel about…" She couldn't say it. Couldn't acknowledge that he'd said he was falling in love with her.

Couldn't *believe* it.

"Wait a minute." He put his hands on her shoulders, trapping her. "I'm not saying I was right to try to date a certain type of woman. I'm just saying that getting over my past tendencies has been a process. And at the other side of the process…" He bent his head to one side and a crooked smile came onto his face. "At the other side of the process, was you."

She bit her lip. "I wasn't just standing here waiting for you, Sam. I'm not going to fall into your arms just because you've figured a few things out."

"And I wouldn't expect you to." He squeezed her shoulders, then let them go and took her hand, urging her to walk a little further. "I know it'll take time and courtship and compromise. I'm just hoping we can do that, is all."

And drat if she didn't still hear that certainty in his voice. She could read his thoughts: *there's no way Susan could say no to me.*

She walked along the dirt road beside him, fuming. This was exactly why she didn't want to get involved with a man. All this scary emotion, all this confusion. All this feeling of hearing his words and trying to interpret what he meant. It made her stomach hurt.

Best to just be alone. She'd always said it,

always known it about herself, and here was exhibit A.

She walked faster.

Until she felt a hand on her shoulder, pressing down, stopping her. "Susan. Wait."

"What?" she asked impatiently without turning around.

Sam stepped in front of her so she couldn't proceed. He looked down at her. "What I really want," he said, "is to kiss you."

She opened her mouth to refuse, and she was going to, for sure. But then she saw that a muscle was twitching under his eye.

Was he nervous?

Sam, the millionaire, nervous?

She cocked her head to one side, looking at him. He'd certainly put on a good show of being the dominant, successful male, but now that she studied him, she could see other signs. The hand he brushed through his hair. The slight uncertainty in his eyes. The way that when his hand reached out to touch her cheek, she could see it trembling just a little.

Now that was different. Sam was so accustomed to putting on a show of confidence in the business world that maybe he didn't know how to conduct himself in the personal world. Maybe he was used to pushing and acting cocky because that's what worked in doing deals. Maybe he didn't know how annoying that trait was when you were trying to declare your feelings to a woman.

"Do you...do you have any of those feelings for me, too?" He was still touching her cheek. And there was still a slight quiver in his hand. "Look, I don't pretend to understand you, or to know exactly how to make this work—"

She reached up and pulled his face down to hers and kissed him.

At least she started to. She started to assume the leadership role, but he quickly took it back, and their connection was a give and take, sweet and intense and...electrifying.

Susan didn't want it to stop, but she felt as if she might pass out if it went on, so she took a step back and stared at him. "Wow."

He nodded slowly, never letting go of her eyes. "Wow."

Then he pulled her to his side and put an arm around her shoulders and they walked together in the direction of the car.

Just like before, only everything was completely different.

Everything was new.

Driving home, the air in the car felt pregnant with possibilities. Susan had never felt anything like those moments with Sam. Not when she was engaged; not on any other dates. Not ever.

And the slight bit of insecurity that he'd shown made her feel as if she knew him better than ever before. That she'd gotten to know another side of the arrogant millionaire. A side she liked better. A side she wanted to know better.

When they pulled up to the house, she wondered if he'd kiss her again. Wondered if her heart could stand it, or if it would race right out of control.

But there was no chance to find out. Because there, sitting in the glow of the headlights, was a familiar figure. "Sam?" she asked, hearing the shrillness at her own voice. "What on earth is my mother doing here?"

Chapter Ten

Still reeling from the intensity of kissing Susan, from the emotions that swelled his heart, Sam climbed out of the car, looking from Susan to her mother and back again. Two more different women could scarcely be imagined.

Where Susan looked funky and individualistic, her mother looked perfectly proper. Hair in a neat, curly style, impeccable makeup, nails done.

He opened the car door for Susan and reached down to help her climb out. Sports cars weren't always the easiest for women to navigate in a dress.

"I'm sorry to just show up here," Mrs. Hayashi said, hurrying toward them, then stopping a few feet away. "I tried to call when I got in to Columbus, but I couldn't get through."

Susan fumbled in her purse for her phone. "I'm sorry, Mom. It was off."

"You've been out? Somewhere dressy?" There were questions in the older woman's voice. "What have you gotten on your shoes, Susie?"

Susan looked down, and so did Sam. "We took a walk," Susan said, coloring deeply.

The two women still hadn't hugged.

Mrs. Hayashi shot him a quick glance, and heat rose in Sam's face, too. Of course, a mother would wonder where her daughter's employer had taken her, and why, and what his intentions were.

If only he knew the answers.

The moon cast a silvery light, making jewels across Susan's dark hair. A chorus of cicadas chirped in rising and falling waves, punctuated by a dog barking somewhere down the road. New-mown grass sent its tangy summer smell from next door.

"Well, I'm forgetting my manners." The woman approached Sam and held out her hand. "I'm Madolyn Hayashi, Susie's mom. It was so kind of you to send me that airline ticket—"

"You *sent* her an *airline* ticket?" Susan's jaw dropped.

"I had the extra miles," Sam tried to explain.

"And I overheard you talking about how you wanted to do that. I just thought I could speed it up a little and give you a nice surprise."

Susan shot him a glare, and he had the feeling that, if her mother weren't here, she'd have kicked him. "Mom," she said, "I was going to send you a ticket next week. I've been saving. You didn't have to take his."

"It was no problem." Sam wasn't sure what he'd done wrong. Was Susan upset that he'd sent her mom a ticket without telling her? Or was it that she didn't want her mom around?

"It was supposed to be for you to take a vacation," Susan went on. "For you to do something relaxing, now that you have a break from Donny."

"Oh, honey, I wanted to see you, not go to a spa!" Almost hesitantly, she stepped closer.

And then the two women lurched into a hug that started out awkward and then lingered long enough to get close. "I missed you so much," Mrs. Hayashi said finally, stepping back to hold Susan's hands. "Especially since Donny's away. I started thinking about things, things I've done wrong."

"Mom…" Susan's face twisted in a complicated expression of love and exasperation and sorrow.

"I know our relationship hasn't been the best, and I wanted to see you, to try to fix things. I had the means, thanks to your boss, so yesterday I just packed up my things and called the airlines, and today…here I am. You don't mind, do you?"

"Mom, I'm glad you're here," Susan said, her eyes shiny in that way Sam was learning meant she was trying not to cry. "If this is where you want to be, I'm glad you came."

Sam had been listening, arms crossed, and thinking at the same time. Susan's mother's words made him reflect about parenting: how quickly it all went by, how little time you really had with your kids. Look at Mindy, away at camp. The first of many times she'd wave and run away. She'd go farther and farther in the years to come.

Susan and her mother had a chance to renew their relationship, right now. And suddenly it came to him, brilliant in its perfect simplicity. "Tell you what," he said, "for once, you *can* have it both ways. There's a spa and resort just an hour away. I have an ownership interest in it, and I'd like to get you two a room and some spa treatments there. You can go pamper yourselves and reconnect."

And the side benefit was that he could figure out what on earth he was doing, kissing Susan.

"No way!" Susan turned away from her mother to face him, hands on hips. "You've already done enough for us, Sam. We couldn't possibly accept."

"I want you to," he said. Even more than with Marie, who'd grown up wealthy, he found he liked providing special things for Susan, who wasn't so used to it. Susan didn't expect people to do things for her; she almost had the reverse of the entitlement mentality he'd seen among so many of his younger workers. "Just take me up on the offer in the spirit it's meant. No obligations, no strings. I just want you to enjoy some time with your mom."

"No!" She was shaking her head. "It's not... we're not..." She lifted her hands, palms up, clearly at a loss to explain.

"Susie." Her mother put a perfectly manicured hand on Susan's shoulder. "It makes him feel good to do it. Men like to do nice things for women."

Susan's eye-roll was monumental, and for just a minute, he could completely picture her as a teenager.

"Let him help us," Mrs. Hayashi urged.

"Besides," Susan went on, twisting away

from her mother in another teenager-like motion, "what about Mindy?"

"I just decided I'm going to take a week off to spend with her. Take her to the zoo, hang out at the pool. I miss her like crazy, having her away for the weekend, and I want to spend some extra time with her."

"That is so sweet," Mrs. Hayashi said. "I think that's wonderful."

Susan obviously didn't share the belief, but the slump of her shoulders let him know she realized she was defeated.

Good. She didn't get enough pampering in her life, that much was obvious.

And time off work would let him do some thinking about where his life was going and what he was doing. He might even go to that men's prayer breakfast Dion and Troy were always bugging him about.

Yes, a week off might give him some more perspective on his life.

"Daddy, I'm gonna listen to Mr. Eakin's story, okay?" Mindy said two evenings later.

"Sure, that's fine."

It was the Senior Towers open house, and the elders had gone all out to get the community to stop in and see what went on there. There

were storytelling and craft booths, a used-book
sale and a table set up to match senior volun-
teers with community needs.

Sam had relished spending the day with
Mindy, hearing her exuberance about her
camping experience, sharing simple summer
pleasures like swimming and cooking out and
the playground in the park.

At the same time, he had to acknowledge
that it was hard to keep a five-year-old enter-
tained. Especially one who was getting super
excited about her upcoming birthday. He had
a renewed respect for teachers and day care
workers and nannies.

And for Susan.

In fact, he'd been thinking a lot about Susan.

Without her, the house was quiet, maybe a
little lonely. There was less color and excitement.

He realized that he missed her in a completely different way than he'd missed Marie.

Marie had been stability and deep married
love. She'd been the mother of his child. And
her death had ripped a hole in his heart and in
their home, one he and Mindy had been struggling to fix ever since.

Susan was excitement and spice. Her absence didn't hurt in the same way that the loss

of Marie had, of course, partly because they knew Susan was coming back, and partly because his and Mindy's relationship with her was just beginning. It wasn't at all clear where it would go.

A lot of that, he realized, depended on him. There was something between him and Susan, something electric. But could he let go of the past for long enough to experience it and see where it led? Could he let go of at least some of his plans for a life as similar as possible to what he and Marie had planned together, what they'd always wanted?

"Sam Hinton." A clawlike hand grasped his arm, and he turned to see Miss Minnie Falcon, his old Sunday school teacher, glaring at him.

"Hey, Miss Minnie," he said. "How are you doing?"

"I'd be more at peace if I knew what was going on over in that mansion of yours."

"What do you mean?"

"I heard you took that nanny of yours out on a date." She looked at him as if he'd pocketed the Sunday school funds.

"I heard the same," came a male voice, one he dreaded because it was always critical and negative. Gramps Camden had issues with Sam's father, but didn't seem to be able to make a distinction between the generations. He always took his ire out on Sam. "Hi, Mr. Camden," Sam said, restraining his sigh.

"What are your intentions toward our Susan?" the older man asked. "I hope you're not taking advantage. She's a real nice girl."

"Yes, she is," Miss Minnie agreed. "Very active in the church. Very helpful, and has a mind of her own."

"Which I wouldn't have figured you to like," Gramps said. "Your father never did."

"Hey, hey," Sam said, trying to still the gossip. "We went out for a friendly dinner. That's all."

"At Chez La Ferme?" Minnie sounded scandalized. "Why, you probably spent over fifty dollars on that dinner. That's hardly something you do with just friends. Or should I say, it's hardly something a poor schoolteacher can afford."

"But a rich businessman can," Gramps said. "Question is, why would he want to?"

"Are you courting her?" Miss Minnie asked.

Sam looked from one to the other and felt a confessional urge similar to one he'd felt years ago, in Sunday school. He gave up trying to say anything but the truth. "I don't know," he admitted. "We're so different. I don't know where it could go, but I do like her."

"How's she feel about you?" Gramps asked. "I warned her about your family. She's probably on her guard, as well she should be."

Sam thought, momentarily, of the way her eyes had softened as he'd leaned down to kiss her. "I think she's as confused as I am."

Miss Minnie frowned. "We've all got our eyes on you, young man."

"And as the man," Gramps said, "it's your job to get yourself un-confused. Figure out what you're doing. Don't string her along."

The old man was right, Sam reflected as he collected Mindy and headed home. The whole town of Rescue River knew what was going on, and he didn't want to cause gossip or hurt Susan's reputation.

He needed to make some decisions, and fast. Before the decisions made themselves for him. He just didn't know what to do.

Susan stood in the giant Rural America Outlet Store with her mother, looking through the little girls' clothing section.

Susan held up a colorful romper. "Mindy would look adorable in this!"

Her mother eyed her speculatively. "You've gotten close to her."

"Even being away for these few days, I've really missed that child." Susan couldn't wait to find out how Mindy had done at camp and to hear her stories of her week with her daddy.

"So get it," her mother said after feeling the fabric and squinting at the price tag. "It's a good bargain. But we should also get her something fun and glittery. Maybe a nail polish set." She led the way out of the clothing department and toward the makeup aisles.

"That's too grown-up," Susan protested, following along past counters of jewelry and watches. "She's only five."

"Turning six, right?" Her mother smiled back at her. "Little girls that age love girly stuff. Even you did, back then."

As they reached the nail polish rack, Susan extended her freshly pedicured foot, showing off her new sparkly pink nail polish. "I did well with the girly stuff this week, didn't I?"

"Kicking and screaming, but yes." Her mother handed her a set of pale colors in a cartoonish box obviously meant for little girls. "What about these?"

Susan studied it. "Well, Sam will shoot me

for buying it, but you're right, Mindy will love some nail polish."

"Then let's get it." Her mother took the polish set from her, checked the price and dropped it into their basket with the satisfied smile of an experienced bargain hunter.

The fun of shopping together was one of many rediscoveries Susan had made during the week. They'd gotten spa treatments and giggled through yoga classes and cried through the sappy chick flicks they both loved. In between, they'd done a little bit of real talking: about Donny, about Susan's father and about the mistakes they'd both made during Susan's stormy adolescence.

One conversation in particular stood out— the one about when Susan's father had left.

"I held onto him long after the love had died," her mother admitted, "with guilt about leaving me with you kids, and with pressure about how he didn't make enough money. I wasn't a good wife, Susie, and after he left, I tried to sway you kids against him."

"You tried so hard to make him happy, though," Susan had protested. "All those Japanese dinners, all your own needs suppressed."

"Which was my choice," Susan's mother declared. "I should have gotten a job and a life, especially after Donny was in school. The truth is, I was depressed and anxious, and I took it out on all of you."

Susan had hugged her mother. "I took out plenty on you, too," she said. "Some of the things I said to you as a teenager! I'm so sorry, Mom."

"Oh, every teenager does that, especially girls. I don't blame you for rebelling."

After that, they'd kept things light, but the tension and awkwardness that had hindered their connection for years was mostly gone. Susan felt better about their relationship than she ever had before, and for that, she was grateful to Sam Hinton.

Twenty minutes after they'd paid for their purchases, they were back at Sam's house, sneaking their bundles past the pool where Sam, Mindy and Mindy's grandparents were setting up for the birthday party that would occur later that day.

"Now, take the time to wrap these nicely," Susan's mother urged as she poured them both sodas. "You know, you really ought to get some decent dishes. You're an adult woman."

"Mindy will rip through this paper in two seconds. It doesn't matter how it looks."

"A nice package, as nice as the other guests

bring, will impress Sam, though," Mom said. "You know, you just might get him to marry you. He's got that look in his eye."

"Mom!"

"He's a great catch," her mother said, coming over to kneel beside the box of wrapping paper Susan was rummaging through. "Look how wealthy and how generous with his money. A good father. You should consider it, sweetie."

Susan felt as if she was choking. "I don't want to do what you did! Look how that turned out!"

Susan's mother's face went sad. "Oh, Susie, it was so complicated between your father and me. You're not going to have the same situation—"

"I don't want to have a marriage that explodes and causes all that pain. I made a decision to stay single, and I'm sticking to it." She was, too. No doubt about it. What had happened between her and Sam, that night of their date, had been temporary insanity.

"Don't be stubborn. You're just like your father in that regard. Just…" Her mother looked off out the window and sighed. "Just choose the right man, the man who truly loves you, who looks at you like you're made of precious gems." She stroked Susan's hair. "And then communicate with him. Don't lose yourself like I did."

"So can I wrap the gift the way I want to?" Susan asked in exasperation.

"It doesn't hurt to show your softer side. You do have one."

So they wrapped the gifts in pink paper, elegantly, to rival Rescue River's finest. And then her mother brushed Susan's hair for her and put a little braid in it.

"You were always the best with my hair, Mom," Susan said, leaning back against her mother's stomach. "I'm so glad you came."

"I'm glad, too." Her mother placed a kiss on top of her head. "And now I'm going to the airport. My van is coming…" She consulted her phone. "Oh my, they're out front now."

"You're leaving already? So soon?"

Her mother clasped her by her shoulders. "You're on your own, you're on your way. You don't need me."

"But I don't want you to go," Susan said, feeling unexpectedly teary.

Sun slanted through the windows. Outside, car doors slammed and excited kids' voices rang out. It sounded as if a lot of people were coming to Mindy's party, and Susan wondered when Sam had planned it. And how he'd managed without her.

Her mother pulled her to her feet. "You have a party to get ready for. Go do that. And come for a visit soon, okay?"

"I will," Susan said. "Let me help carry your bags."

Her mother waved the offer aside. "I only have one bag, and I left it downstairs. Go get ready for your party."

Susan opened her arms, and her mother came to her in a fierce hug that made them both cry a little. And then her mother gave a jaunty wave and hurried down the stairs.

Party noise drifted through the screen door, and all of a sudden, Susan didn't want to be out of the action anymore. She needed to be a part of this important day in Sam and Mindy's life.

She changed into shorts and a sleeveless blouse, and hurried down the stairs, and immediately understood how Sam had gotten the party planned so fast.

Helen was greeting the well-dressed parents and children, and Ralph was directing a truck containing two ponies to an appropriate unloading spot—the pad behind the garage, where Susan kept her car.

Susan walked slowly toward the gathering, holding her nicely wrapped gift, which suddenly seemed cheap. Uncertainty clawed at her, and then she saw Mindy.

Mindy spotted her at the same time and started running. What could Susan do but kneel down and open her arms?

"There you are! I knew you'd come back in time!" she crowed, loud enough for everyone to hear. "Grandma and Daddy said you might not, but I knew you would!"

"I wouldn't miss it, sweetheart," Susan said, burying her nose in the sweaty, baby-shampoo scent of Mindy's hair.

"Guess what! I got my new little dog! Only," Mindy said frowning, "Uncle Troy said we had to shut her upstairs in her crate cuz the party's too much excitement for her. But that's only while she's a new dog."

So he'd gotten her a dog. *Good job, Sam.* "I can't wait to see her! Maybe after the party."

"You know what?" Mindy said in a serious voice, as if she was figuring something out. "You know what I really want for my birthday?"

The intensity of Mindy's voice had most of the others quieting down to hear.

"What, honey?" Susan asked.

Mindy put a hand on her hip and touched Susan's face with her half arm. "I want *you* to be my new mommy!"

Chapter Eleven

Sam heard his daughter's words ring out, clear as a bell. *I want you to be my new mommy.* So, apparently, did everyone else at the party, because a hush fell over the yard.

He knew who his daughter was talking to without even looking. Susan.

The silence was replaced by the buzz of adult conversation that seemed to include a fair share of gossip and curious glances.

He looked toward where he'd heard Mindy's voice and saw that Susan had squatted down in front of her, talking quickly, smiling and laughing, redirecting Mindy's attention to the modest gift in her hand, to the clown who was setting up shop in the driveway.

We have a clown? Sam thought blankly.

Mindy was smiling and laughing as Susan

talked to her, so that was all right. Mindy's words had to have been embarrassing to Susan, since everyone had heard, but as usual, her focus had gone immediately to Mindy and making sure she was okay and handling it.

In the direction of the pool area, he heard the sound of sniffling and turned to see his mother-in-law fumbling for a napkin and wiping her eyes. She wasn't one to break down, especially when she had a party to run, but Mindy's words had obviously struck a nerve.

They'd struck a nerve in him, too. Trust a little kid to lay out everything so baldly and clearly. She wanted a new mommy. And she'd decided she wanted Susan.

Which had to go totally against Helen's grain. He strode over to see what he could do for his grieving mother-in-law.

Former mother-in-law.

As he bent to put an arm around Helen, he caught Susan studying him, her eyes thoughtful.

Sam blew out a breath. Everything was coming to a head now. Mindy, Helen, Susan. It was an emotional triangle he couldn't figure out how to manage, couldn't fix. He, who could easily run a complex business, had no idea what to do, no idea how to arrange his personal life.

"Helen, you don't want to make a scene in front of all of these folks," said Ralph, patting his wife's arm and looking every bit as confused as Sam felt.

"You get those ponies set up," Helen snapped at her husband. "I have to talk to Sam."

After making sure that everyone had access to food and drink, and that Lou Ann Miller was supervising any kids who wanted to swim, Sam led Helen to the shelter beside the pool house. Bushes blocked it from the rest of the house and there was some privacy.

"Hey," he said once he'd got her seated on a picnic bench and found her a can of soda and a napkin to blow her nose. "You're going to be okay." He was terrible at this, terrible at comforting. He remembered all the times he'd tried and failed to comfort Marie. The one thing he'd been able to do to make her feel better, at the end of her life, was the promise. The promise that now dragged at his soul.

"You promised!" It was as if Helen read his mind. "Sam, you promised you'd marry someone like her, someone who would fulfill her legacy. And instead you've come up with... that woman."

"I don't know where the relationship with Susan is going," Sam said truthfully, all of a sudden realizing that he did, in fact, have a relationship with her.

"That woman can't cook, she wants to work rather than staying home, and she says the wrong thing all the time. She's so...different."

"That's for sure," Sam agreed. "Susan is different."

"Marie would hate her!"

Sam thought about it and decided that, yes, it was probably true. Marie would at least be made very insecure by Susan. But Marie *was* insecure, and that was what had made her such a perfectionist. And her insecurity had everything to do with her mother's demanding standards.

He didn't want to raise Mindy like that.

"She'd be a horrible mother. And you promised you'd marry someone like Marie."

Sam sighed heavily. "It's true. If I want to keep my promise to Marie, I...I can't marry Susan." As he said it, he felt trapped in a cage made of his own beliefs, the beliefs he'd always held about what made a good marriage, a good home, a good life.

Desperate for freedom, he lifted his head

from his hands…and saw Susan and Mindy standing in the shelter's gateway.

And from the look on Susan's face, she'd overheard every word.

She squatted down and whispered something to Mindy. As Mindy ran toward him and Helen, Susan turned and left, almost at a run.

"Come on, Daddy, the kids all want to ride ponies and swim and nobody knows what to do!"

He had to take control of his child's party. He stood and walked out, feeling dazed, looking for Susan. But she was nowhere to be seen.

Susan's world spun as she thought about what she'd overheard. *I can't marry Susan. Marie would hate her.*

She fell backward on her bed, staring up at the ceiling, eyes dry, stomach cold. She lay there for a long time while the sounds of the ongoing party drifted up to her.

It's fine, she told herself. It wasn't as if he'd proposed.

But if he'd made some kind of promise about what kind of woman to marry—and who made that kind of promise, anyway?—then what was he doing kissing her?

It was like her dad, saying one thing and doing another. Men were so unreliable.

And what of what Helen had said, about how bad she was at household duties? Hadn't she proven that to be true?

Just like her ex-fiancé, Sam didn't want a woman like her.

Her foolish dreams crashed down around her and she squeezed her eyes shut, willing herself not to cry. She was a strong woman, and she would survive this. After just a little period of mourning.

Her phone buzzed with a text from Daisy. Where are you?

Susan ignored it. Clicked off her phone.

The ache in her chest was huge, as if someone had dug a hole there with a blunt shovel. It hurt so much that she couldn't move, couldn't think. *God, help*, she prayed, unable to find more words.

In response, she felt a small soothing rush of love.

She'd always gone to church, read her Bible when there was a study group to push her, talked over her questions with friends like Daisy. She'd felt God's call for her vocation as a teacher. She knew she was saved.

But she'd never thought much about being

loved by God. She'd never *felt* it, not deep inside. Now, the small soothing trickle grew to a warm glow.

Her father had only loved her conditionally, and he'd abandoned her. They spoke rarely by phone, and only at his instigation. Never when she needed him.

Her heavenly Father was different. He was here, waiting for her to reach out. *Rest in me*, He seemed to say.

Her hurt about Sam didn't evaporate. In fact, knowing God loved her seemed to unfreeze the tears, and they trickled down the sides of her face and into her hair. She'd never have a future with Sam and Mindy, and the cold truth of that stabbed into her like an icicle, letting her know that somewhere inside, she'd been nursing a dream to life.

Now that dream was pierced, deflated, gone.

Finally, a long while later, she dragged herself out of bed and looked out the window. Most of the kids were inside, no doubt eating birthday cake. The clown was packing up to go. He'd removed his red wig and rubbery nose, but his smile was still painted on.

She watched him pack his clown supplies into his rusty car trunk. He looked tired.

Could she keep a smile pasted on in the face of what she'd heard?

No.

She pulled out her suitcase and hauled a couple of boxes out of the closet. She opened the suitcase on her bed.

She'd started to dream, to hope. Crazy, stupid hope.

And a little girl would suffer because of it. "I want you to be my new mommy," Mindy had said earlier today, and the words, and the notion, had thrilled Susan way too much.

But she could never, ever be Mindy's new mommy. Because Sam had made a promise.

She opened her dresser drawers and started throwing clothes randomly into the suitcase, blinking against the tears that kept blurring her vision. From the open window, she heard car doors slamming, adults calling to one another. The parents were starting to arrive. The party was almost over.

She heard steps coming up the porch stairs, double time. "There you are!" Mindy said, rushing in. "Come see all my presents!" Then she seemed to notice something on Susan's face. She stopped still and looked around the room. "Whatcha doing?"

Susan's heart was breaking. Rip the bandage off quickly, she told herself. "I have to go away," she said.

"But you just got back from a trip."

"No, I mean…I can't stay here anymore."

"Why not?"

Why not indeed, when she loved this little girl almost as much as she loved her difficult, obstinate father? "It's just not working out. But I'll still see you lots, honey. I'll see you at school."

"I don't want you to go."

Susan couldn't help it; she knelt to hug the little girl. "I'm sorry, honey. I don't want to go either, but it's for the best."

Mindy's shoulders shook a little, but she didn't sob out loud. So she was starting to learn self-control. Growing up more each day.

Susan hugged the child tighter, but she struggled out of Susan's arms and ran down the stairs without looking back.

"Whoa there!" came Sam's voice, drifting up through the windows. "C'mere, sweetie. What's wrong?"

Panic rose in Susan at the thought of facing Sam. She needed to get this done fast. She'd just take a few things for now and send for the rest, because staying to pack and move would be too painful. Maybe this way, she could avoid seeing Sam or upsetting Mindy again.

She didn't even have an idea of where to go. Maybe to the little motel in outside of town, until she could figure something else out. Maybe she could go spend the rest of the summer with her mom, drop in unexpectedly just as Mom had done on her.

Heavy steps climbed the wooden stairs, and there was a knock on the open screen door. "Susan?"

She sucked in a breath. Sam. She'd moved too slowly, lost her chance of easy escape. "Come in," she said, feeling as if she was made of stone.

"What's going on here?" he asked, stopping at the door of her bedroom.

"I'm leaving."

"Why?"

What could she say? Because I've fallen in love with you and staying will break my heart? And Mindy's heart, too, because it can't be permanent?

Men were not dependable. She'd always known it, but for a while, Sam had seemed to defy the norm. But he'd proven, too, that he couldn't be trusted, that she'd be better off alone.

"It's just not working out," she said, and found the strength from somewhere to snap her suitcase closed.

He stood in the doorway as if he was frozen there.

She had to leave now or she'd never be able to. "Excuse me," she said, and slipped sideways past him. She trotted out the door and down the stairs.

Sam didn't know how long he stood there after Susan left. But finally standing got to be too much of an effort and he sank down onto her bed. Collapsed down to rest his head on her pillow. Inhaled her scent of honeysuckle, and his throat tightened.

Why had she gone? Was it just that she was flighty, transient, easily bored? Had his and Mindy's life proven too dull for her? Now that she'd earned enough money to send her brother to camp and make things up with her mom, had she gotten everything she could out of him?

But that *wasn't* it. Or at least, it wasn't all. She'd overheard what he'd said to Helen, and it had hurt her.

Having her gone had been bad enough when

it was just for a week, but the expression on her face when she'd left had suggested that this time, it was permanent. She'd left for good.

Maybe she was oversensitive. Maybe he'd been right: he needed to stick to his kind of woman. Someone solid and stable and from his background. Someone who valued home and family over excitement. Someone who was in it for the long haul.

But the idea of finding someone else, a clone of the stable, boring blondes he'd dated over the past year, made him squeeze his eyes shut in despair.

He didn't want that. But he'd made a promise.

He was well and truly trapped.

"Hey, Sam!" He heard voices calling outside the window at the same time his cell phone buzzed.

He didn't have the energy to pick it up, but his wretched sense of duty made him look at the screen. Daisy. He texted back a question mark, having no heart for more.

Is Mindy with you? she texted.

He hit the call button, and Daisy answered immediately. "Do you have Mindy?"

"No. She was down on the driveway a few minutes ago."

"Well, everyone's gone, and I don't see her anywhere."

Sam stood and strode to the window. He scanned the yard. He didn't see her, either.

He did see Susan's car. Susan and Daisy were standing by it together. So she hadn't left yet.

"I'm on my way down," he said, and clicked off the phone.

Susan followed Daisy back into the house she'd thought she was leaving forever.

"Maybe she just fell asleep somewhere," Daisy was saying. "Or maybe Troy and Angelica took her home? Would they do that? I'll call them."

She was starting to place the call when Susan put a hand on her friend's arm. "I think I know why she's missing," she said. "It's my fault."

"What?"

So she filled Daisy in on the skeleton details of how she'd been packing and Mindy had found her and gotten upset.

"I'm going to want to hear more about this later," Daisy said, "but for now, let's find Mindy."

A quick survey of the house revealed nothing. They'd already checked the pool, of course, but they went back to look around the pool house. The place where Susan had heard about Sam's promise. Where he'd broken her heart. But there was no time for self-indulgence now.

My prickly independence hurt a little girl, she thought as she searched the woods at the edge of Sam's property. *I need to do something about that. If only I hadn't just run up and packed, Mindy wouldn't be missing.*

They checked in with Sam, who was white-faced and tight-lipped, searching the property lines as well. Phone calls were made, and within minutes Fern and Carlo, Troy and Angelica came back, with Lou Ann Miller to watch Mercy and Xavier.

"I shouldn't have jumped into packing," Susan lamented as she, Fern and Angelica walked back into the fields behind Sam's property, calling Mindy's name. "I always think I'm just going to run away. If I hadn't done that, she wouldn't be missing."

Fern patted her arm. "Don't forget the time Mercy went missing. Only it was the dead of winter out at the skating pond. I totally blamed myself, but I've come to realize these things happen. We'll find her."

"It's true," Angelica said, giving her a quick side-arm hug. "Don't blame yourself. We all make mistakes with kids."

"You guys are the best," Susan said, gripping each of their hands, not bothering to hide her tears. She couldn't even pretend to be an island now. She needed her friends.

They met up with the men and Daisy in front of the house. "She just can't have gotten far," Troy was saying. "Look, Angelica and I will head to the surrounding houses."

"We'll check the library and the downtown," Carlo said, "just in case she took off running."

Sam shook his head. "I have this feeling she's somewhere in the house. I'm going to search this place from top to bottom. But let's get Dion involved, just in case."

At that, Susan's heart twisted. Everyone else looked half-sick, too, reminded of what could happen to missing little girls.

Daisy made the call to Dion, and then she, Susan and Sam started methodically going through the house. Susan realized anew how huge it was, how many spots there were for a little girl to hide. They searched each floor together, checking in with the other searchers.

Dion came in his cruiser and drove the neighborhoods.

The basement yielded nothing, and the main floor didn't, either. Susan thought she saw a head of blond hair in the playroom, but it was just a doll.

Upstairs, they went through Mindy's bedroom and all the closets, and then started on the spare bedrooms. Nothing.

But as they headed back downstairs, Susan heard a sound, like a sob, behind the sunroom door, that mysterious door that always remained closed.

"Did you hear that?" she asked.

"What? Where?"

Susan indicated the closed door.

"She wouldn't go in there," Sam said. "She's scared of it, because—" He broke off.

"Didn't you ever change it?" Daisy looked at Sam.

"Not yet," he said, and opened the door.

Inside was a beautiful, multi-windowed sunroom with wicker furniture and a rattan carpet, decorated in rust and brown and cream. Autumn colors.

In the center of the room was a hospital bed.

In a flash it came to Susan: this must be the place where Marie had died.

There was a bump in the covers of the bed. And there, sleeping restlessly, with the occasional hiccupping sob, was Mindy. Her new little black-and-white dog slept in her arms.

They all three looked at each other. Daisy bit her lip, tears in her eyes. "You have to get rid of that bed, Sam. You have to open this place up."

He nodded without speaking, and from the way his throat was working, Susan could see that he could barely restrain tears, himself.

"Thank the Lord we found her." Daisy hugged both of them.

Sam picked Mindy up and carried her to her bedroom while Daisy and Susan called the others.

"Now, what's this about you packing? Why were you leaving?" Daisy asked as they walked out to meet the others.

Fern fell into step beside them.

"It's time for girl talk," Daisy told her. "Susan was thinking of leaving."

Fern winced. "I remember when you guys talked sense into me," she said. She beckoned to Angelica, and the four of them headed into the living room, which looked to be the most secluded place right now.

"It's not that I need sense talked into me,"

Susan said, sinking into one of the formal living room chairs. She was too broken down to lie or conceal her feelings. "I love him. And I love Mindy. But he's never going to be able to commit to someone like me. I heard him say it." She shrugged. "I guess I'm just too different from him, not his type."

"Do I look like Carlo's type?" Fern asked. "I'm a librarian, and he's a mercenary, or at least he used to be. What could we have in common? But love is strange."

Angelica leaned forward and took Susan's hand. "It's hard to trust in men after you've been hurt," she said. "But it's so, so worth it."

"Just stay a little longer," Daisy urged. "Talk to Sam."

Susan wanted to take in what they were saying, but her heart was aching and her head was confused.

They talked a few minutes longer, and then Troy and Carlo called from the foyer and everyone started to leave.

Susan stayed, alone, sitting on the couch in the gathering darkness, too drained to move. "Thank You for letting us find her, Father," she prayed. "I'm sorry I'm so messed up. Please, help me to change so I can find love and do what's important."

She sat without tuning on a lamp, listening to the murmur of Sam talking to Dion on the porch, feeling alternating waves of sadness and God's healing love wash over her.

Finally, she curled up on her side on the narrow couch, tucked a hard, uncomfortable pillow beneath her head, and fell asleep.

Chapter Twelve

Sam sank down onto the wicker armchair on the front porch, waving to Troy and Angelica as they drove away, tooting their horn.

Only Dion remained, his cruiser parked out on the street. "You okay, my man?"

Sam stared out at the night sky. "Not really."

"Rough day." Dion sat down in the other chair, propped his hands behind his head and put his feet up on the wicker coffee table. "Now's the time you wish for a woman to bring you a tall iced tea."

"Tea's in the refrigerator," Sam offered. "I think."

"Exactly. That would require effort."

They sat together for a few minutes in a comfortable silence.

"Sorry I made you search the streets,"

Sam said finally. "Mindy never goes in the sunroom."

"The room where your wife died?"

Sam nodded. "I...just keep the door closed."

Dion nodded, tipping the chair back on two legs. "I did that for a while myself. At the house we shared, and in my heart."

"And you stopped? How?"

Dion shrugged, still staring out into the gathering darkness. "Time, man. Time, and prayer." He leveled a stern look at Sam. "You've had enough time, but you could use some help on the prayer side."

"I'm coming to the men's breakfast," Sam protested.

"Which I'm glad of. But you might need a private consult with the Lord."

Sam smiled at the terminology. "I know I do."

"Marie was a good woman," Dion said, and then paused.

Sam knew a "but" was coming. "But what?"

"But I'm guessing she must've been a little hard to live with."

A few weeks ago, that remark would have surprised him and roused his defenses. Now he just nodded. "She was pretty tense."

"Grew up that way, I guess."

"Exactly." Sam thought about his in-laws. Marie had never really broken away from them enough to have her own life. Everything had been colored by their insistence on perfection, on image. It wasn't that they were bad people, just a little misguided about what was important. "They were…controlling."

"Sounds like someone I know."

"What?"

"Look in the mirror, my man." Dion gave him a look. "Everyone knows you're a dominant alpha-jerk. It's a wonder you have so many friends."

He knew he was controlling, but he'd never put it all together like that. "Is that why Marie married me?"

Dion spread his hands, palms up. "I hate to say it, but she kind of married her mother."

"Hey!"

Dion stood up, clapped him hard on the back. "Think about it, my man. How long you gonna force yourself to live in the past? Don't you remember you can be a new creation?"

And he waved and headed down the long front walk to his cruiser.

Restless, Sam stood and went inside. He checked on Mindy, who was sleeping peacefully, her new little dog beside her. The rule he'd made, no dogs in bed, was obviously not going to stick.

And then he went downstairs to the room where they'd found her. Marie's room. Or Mommy's room, as they'd called it when Marie was alive.

He sat in the chair where he'd spent so much time, right beside the hospital bed where she'd lain as the strength had slowly left her body. Talking to her, trying to cheer her up, reading with her, watching the house and garden shows she'd loved.

Even though the shows had bored him to tears, he'd kept watching them religiously for the first year after her death, because he'd felt closer to her that way. But, he realized, he hadn't seen one in six or eight months.

Dion was right. There came a time to move on.

He leaned forward, elbows on knees, hands clasped together. It was a prayer position, but he wasn't talking to God, not yet. He was talking to Marie. Telling her how sad he was that their dream hadn't worked out. How sorry that he'd been a controlling replica of her parents, that he hadn't encouraged her to spread her wings and fly. Letting her know that he couldn't keep the promise he'd made.

After a while, he stopped telling her anything and just sat. Just invoked the Lord's presence, asking for help. Confessing his sins there, too.

And as he sat, in prayerful meditation, a realization came to him.

Marie was with Christ. He'd prepared for her a room in His mansion. He'd promised that He'd see her face to face.

Oh, Sam had known that, but he hadn't *known* it. Hadn't really felt it.

Marie was happy now, happier than she'd ever been in life. Free of her failing body. Free of her insecurities. Free to love.

Marie had moved on to a new life, one he couldn't even imagine.

And likewise, she hadn't been able to imagine that he would move on, that life would change, that Mindy would grow beyond toddlerhood and would maybe need something, and someone, new. Maybe Sam would, too.

With the promises of Christ, Sam could move on, just as Marie had.

He sat until the tears had mostly stopped falling. Grabbed a tissue from the box Marie had always kept by her bed, a box that hadn't been used or changed out since she'd died.

He wiped his face and blew his nose and felt like an idiot, but a cleansed one. A healed one.

He took a deep breath, opened the door wide and went to find Susan.

Earlier, he'd seen that Susan's car was still behind the garage apartment. She hadn't left with Daisy, so she must have gone back to stay in her apartment. Which was good, because he had things he wanted to say to her.

But the apartment was dark, and she wasn't there, and fear gripped his heart.

What if she'd found another ride, sometime when he wasn't looking? What if she'd left? Left, before he could tell her all the things he wanted to tell her?

He walked back into the house, exhaustion hitting him hard. It had been a long and stressful day, full of fear and joy, sadness and closure. What he wanted at the end of this long day—at the end of any long day—was to be with the woman he loved. But she wasn't here.

As Sam walked through the house, hoping to hear Susan's voice, he seemed to see it with new eyes. It had been Marie's pride and joy; she'd loved inviting her friends here, serving tea, hosting her book club. At one time, the place had been his dream, too, full of stability and love, a home base that ran as smoothly as a business.

Now, it felt empty, lifeless, sad. Was this even the house he wanted to live in? Was it the right place for Mindy to grow up, formal as it was and full of sad memories?

Desolation gripped him hard.

He felt like just collapsing into bed, but he had responsibilities. He finished his walk-through of the house, just as he did every night, shutting off lights, locking doors, checking to make sure nothing was amiss. He picked up some cups and a few stray cupcake wrappers that remained from the party. Feeling utterly alone.

And then he saw her.

Curled up on the couch like a young girl, her fist at her mouth, silky black hair spread over her shoulders. In sleep, the determination and spark and movement weren't there, and she looked totally vulnerable.

Totally lovely.

Joy was surging in his heart that she hadn't left him, that she was still in the house. She was still in reach. There was a chance.

He pulled up an ottoman and sat beside her, but just watching her sleep felt creepy. So he touched her arm, patted her awake. "Hey."

She opened her eyes slowly, and Sam got a momentary vision of what it might be like to watch her wake up every day. His heart ached with longing to be the man who saw that, who was there with her.

"I fell asleep," she said, looking around. "What time is it?"

"It's late," he said. "Ten or so."

Susan stretched and pushed herself up into a semi-reclining position, propped on pillows, rubbing her arms.

"You're cold," he said, and looked for an afghan or throw. Finding none, he went to the front closet and found one of his sweatshirts. "Here," he said, tucking it gently around her shoulders.

She blinked. "What time did you say it was? And hey, are we even allowed to put our feet on this couch?"

"We are now," he said.

She grabbed her phone and studied it. "If I go now, I can get a seat." She started to stand up.

"Wait. What seat?"

"On a plane to California," she said, putting her feet down and brushing her hands over her messy hair. "There's this online standby thing, and it looks like I have a seat if I can claim it by eleven. I've got to go."

He put a hand on her knee. "Susan. Wait."

"If you're going to yell at me, don't bother. I already know I made a mess of things." She was fumbling for her shoes, checking her phone again, looking anywhere but his face.

"What did you make a mess of?"

She stopped fussing and looked at him. "It was because of me that Mindy hid," she said. "She found me packing and got upset. I think she felt like it was another mother figure leaving her alone." She shook her head rapidly. "I'm so sorry I did that to her."

"Why were you packing to leave?" If it was because she didn't care, then he had to let her go.

"Because," she said slowly, "Because I heard what you said to Helen. That you could never marry me, that you made a promise."

"Ah." He took her hands. "I was afraid that was the problem." And he explained about the promise.

"You're right that I'm never going to be that person," she said. "And I don't want to break Mindy's heart. Or mine. I need to go now, before we get more attached."

"Wait." He shook his head slowly. "I've realized something now. That promise is something that helped me to grieve, stopped me from moving on too soon. But it doesn't hold now. It's like the old law and the new."

"What do you mean?" She sounded troubled.

"Susan, one thing you've helped me see is that I needed to change. I don't have an easy time with change, never have. I'm the steady, boring, rock-solid type."

One side of her mouth quirked up. "Never boring. And steady's not so bad."

"Steady is okay, but I've seen that change is part of life. There's a new way. I'm a new creation."

She raised an eyebrow. "You mean like a new creation in Christ? You're talking religious, and that's not like you."

"It's like me now," he said. "I've recommitted. I've stopped blaming Him for what happened. With God's help, I'm back."

"Oh, Sam, I'm so happy for you!" She threw her arms around him.

Susan felt happy for Sam and more peaceful for herself, but she still had to get going. She talked to Sam for a few minutes, hearing about his conversation with Dion, glad to know he was getting right with the Lord.

But seeing his handsome face lose some of its tension, seeing the light in his eyes that hadn't been there before, just made him more attractive.

"Look," she said finally, "this is wonderful, but I really have to go. If I start driving in the next ten minutes, I can get to the airport just in time to catch this flight."

His lips tightened, but he nodded and followed her to the door. "Your purse, your phone?" he said, looking out for her, making sure she had what she needed.

She swallowed hard as she walked out of the house, because this was truly goodbye. "I'll send for my stuff," she said.

His hands clapped down on her shoulders, turning her to face him. Behind him, his giant mansion shone in the moonlight.

The mansion that had become home to her.

Looking up at him, thinking of Mindy in the house behind him, just about broke her heart.

"I don't want you to go. I want you to stay."

She shook her head. "It's just hurting Mindy," she said. "And me."

"Why is it hurting you?" he asked, touching her chin to make her look at him.

He was going to make her say it, but what did it matter now? She was already hurting and she was leaving. "Because I've fallen in love with you and Mindy. With this life we're playing at. I want to have it for real, but I can't."

"Why not? Susan, what you just said makes me the happiest man in the world." He sank down to his knees. "I want to marry you. I don't know how or when, I know Mindy and I have a little more healing work to do, but I think we can do it with your help. I want you to be Mindy's new mommy. And my wife. Especially my wife."

"But your promise to Marie…"

He shook his head. "I've made my peace with that. With her. I'm not held to it any more."

"For real?" She wanted to believe it, but she wasn't sure she could trust him. Was he just saying that? Could people really heal from a loss like the one he and Mindy had sustained?

"I am completely, totally sure." He swept her into his arms and carried her over to the lawn swing she'd insisted they get.

"Sam!"

"No near neighbors to see," he said. "And I want to prove to you just how much I love you."

He cradled her against his chest and kissed

her tenderly, and Susan's last shreds of doubt wafted away on the gentle night breeze. Eagerly, she kissed him back and then stroked his hair and looked into his eyes.

"Does that mean yes?" he asked, sounding a little insecure.

She laughed out loud. "When does the nanny ever say no to the millionaire?"

"This is a serious moment!" He shook his head, then traced a finger along her cheek. "And I take nothing for granted."

"I'm sorry," she giggled, her heart almost bursting with joy, her soul singing. Daisy had been right: God's plan for her, for all of them, was bigger and deeper and richer than their human minds could imagine. "I'm just so happy. And it's totally a yes."

Epilogue

"I can't believe you let her do a beauty pageant," Susan said as she and Sam approached the Rescue River community center, hand in hand. Mindy ran ahead of them, wearing a poufy pink dress and scuffed cowboy boots.

Sam chuckled. "It's a different kind of pageant, you'll see."

Susan looked around at other families approaching with their daughters of various ages. Some were dressed in customary pageant gear, but others wore shorts or jeans. Susan noticed one girl in a traditional Chinese cheongsam dress and two other girls, one looking Indian and the other redheaded, wearing matching saris.

"The main rule is that the girls wear what they like. Mindy feels beautiful in that dress. But they're not judged on how they look."

"Then what are they judged on?"

"You'll see."

"I'll take your word for it," Susan said, snuggling closer to Sam's side. "I know it makes her grandma happy, so I'm glad we're here." In the two months since they'd declared their love for each other, Susan had been learning a lot about compromise and communication— and about being loved for exactly who she was.

"Look," Mindy cried, "They have crafts! And I see Miss Fern!"

Sam and Susan followed Mindy to an area where several tables stocked with art supplies were set up. The directions, printed large and bold, instructed participants to make art about something they wanted to do when they were older.

"Hey," Fern greeted them as she pulled out a huge sheet of paper. "You've got plenty of time, honey," she said as she handed it to Mindy. "Make whatever you like, just something you want to do when you're older. There are other art tables with other topics, when you're done here. Do you want a smock to cover that pretty dress?"

Mindy plunged her arms into a smock and sat down beside Fern's daughter, who was vigorously painting.

"Looks like Dad's one of the judges again," Sam observed, looking toward the stage where the judges' tables were being set up. "Last year, he almost came to blows with Gramps Camden."

Helen approached, brushing a hand over her granddaughter's shoulders before turning to Sam and Susan. "We put Lou Ann Miller in between. We're hoping that keeps everyone on good behavior. Hi, Susan."

"Hi." Susan returned the wary greeting and then, impulsively, hugged the older woman. They were starting to forge a relationship, but it would be a slow process. "You were right," Susan said, determined to do her part. "She does look beautiful in her dress, and this is a great event for girls."

When they released the hug and stepped back, Helen's eyes were shiny. "I just want Mindy to be happy," she said. "And I want to be a part of her life."

"Of course you do. You're a huge part of her life, and you always will be."

After an hour of mingling and following Mindy from art table to art table, the formal ceremony began. Susan sat back and listened, impressed, to the girls of all ages talking about the required topics, sometimes displaying art to go alongside. Finally, it was Mindy's turn, and as she walked confidently up to the stage, Sam gripped Susan's hand.

It was as if she could read his mind: he was nervous for Mindy, wanting her to do well, wanting her to feel good about it. Susan felt the same way. She loved the little girl more each day.

"Something I did that was hard," Mindy said into the microphone, speaking clearly, "was I went into my mommy-who-died's room. I used to be scared in there but now I'm not cuz I have my puppy." She held up a picture of Bonz. "I went in there and was brave to tell my mommy who died that I want a new mommy, and she said it was okay."

There was a collective sigh and a spontaneous round of applause.

"And something I like to do," Mindy said, "is hug people. I can hug just as good as anybody else even though I just have one hand."

Another collective "aww."

"I want to show that, for this pageant, but I have to get my daddy and my Miss Susan to come up here," she said, "cuz they're gonna get married."

Gasps and murmurs filled the room, and

Sam looked at Susan. "Guess the secret's out. You game?"

"Of course." It had been an open secret, really; in a town like Rescue River, you couldn't hide a relationship very well.

So they went up front and Mindy proved that she could, indeed, hug as well as anyone else. And as the applause swelled for the three of them, standing there hugging each other tightly, Susan felt the invisible Master who'd been guiding them together from the beginning, and looked up through tears to offer praise.

* * * * *

Dear Reader,

Welcome back to Rescue River! I hope you enjoyed Sam and Susan's romance as much as I enjoyed writing it...once I got my matchmaking right! You see, I originally paired Sam with another heroine, a nanny from out of town, but she just didn't have the backbone to stand up to stubborn, bossy Sam. I started thinking about what kind of woman would be perfect for him...and when I realized it was Susan, the whole story fell into place. Susan has been a part of the Rescue River series from the beginning; she was Xavier's teacher in *Engaged to the Single Mom* and shy Fern's friend in *His Secret Child*. She's not perfect, and she knows it, but she's perfect for Sam.

Hmm...wonder who's next to fall in love in Rescue River? Please stop by my website, *leetobinmcclain.com*, to sign up for my newsletter. You'll get information about new releases as well as a free romance story.

Thank you for reading, and may God pour out His rich blessings on you and those you love.

Lee